Hi Lauren

FORMER.LY

DANE COBAIN

Hope you enjoy! :)

Cover Design by Dane Cobain
Edited by Pam Harris

*This is a work of fiction. Names, characters, places, brands, media, and incidents are either the product
of the author's imagination or are used fictitiously. Any resemblance to similarly named places or to
persons living or deceased is unintentional.*

CHAPTER ONE

"ONE HUNDRED and forty-six thousand, three hundred and fifty-seven people die every day. That's six thousand and ninety-nine an hour, one hundred and two a minute or five every three seconds. Over fifty million people every year. How about that for a target audience?"

Looking back, I should've anticipated an unorthodox interview. I mean, how do you deal with a man who reduces human life and death to numbers and statistics? And once you learn to deal with him, how do you laugh, talk, eat, live and work with him? Tech start-ups are notorious for their crazy founders, but John Mayers took the biscuit.

"Welcome to Former.ly," my potential boss announced, gesturing to the chaotic room around him. "Sorry about the mess. We don't have many visitors."

"I wonder why," I mumbled. The office looked more like a frat house. The place reeked of stale beer and sweat, and a pile of stinking clothes shuddered and then sat upright. It lifted a crusty hand in acknowledgement and said something vague about caffeine.

"That's Kerry," said John. "He's our video guy. He's a useless bastard, but give him a camera and he's a machine. Morning, Kerry!"

"Morning, dude," he replied, shuffling out of his rags and into a semi-respectable pair of khaki shorts, flashing a glimpse of oversized thighs and off-white Y-fronts. He grabbed a starched Hawaiian shirt from the floor in front of the sofa, sniffed it to determine its freshness, and pulled it over his head. Then, he hobbled over to meet us in the middle of the debris-strewn living room. He smelled even worse up close, somewhere between a cesspit and a brewery. "Don't ask. It's still rendering. I'm going to grab a shower."

"Yeah, yeah," John replied. "He always says that. Sometimes I wonder what we pay him for."

I watched Kerry retreat through a narrow doorway as John cleared a space for me on the sofa. I didn't really want to sit on it, but I didn't have much of a choice. It crunched as I sat down; sofas aren't meant to do that.

"So," John said, clapping his hands together. "Let's get straight to business. After all, we're both men of business when all is said and done. Tell me what you know about our company."

"Not much," I laughed, nervously.

"I can see that," John said. "You're wearing a suit for a start. But you must have looked us up before you applied to join the team."

"Well," I replied. "I know the basic mechanics – you sign up, you post updates which are hidden from view, and then when you die, your profile goes live to the public."

"That's all you need to know. We plan to monetise death, Dan." As he spoke, a key turned in the latch and the front door opened, letting in the cold and the distant sound of traffic. "We're looking for a front-end developer, and you more than fit the bill in terms of qualifications and experience. But what about culture? Dedication? Think you can match us there? Hey, Flick."

I turned to look at the newcomer, a pretty blonde woman who strolled into the room, pulled a MacBook Air from a tartan satchel and prepared to start work. She smiled sweetly at the two men who faced her.

"Morning, John," she said. "Abhi's here too. He's just parking the car."

"Good lad. When he comes in, tell him to come and meet Dan. He's here about the developer job."

"Hi, Dan," she said, as she logged into her machine. "I'm Felicity, but everyone calls me Flick."

"Hi, Flick," I replied. "Nice to meet you. What's your role? You don't look like a typical programmer."

"Thanks! That's probably because I'm not a programmer. I just do whatever needs doing. I'm in charge of PR and office management, but I spend half of my time cleaning this place up and half of my time looking after the boys. That doesn't leave room for much else."

"How do you fit it all in?" I asked.

"I do a lot of unpaid overtime," she replied. "And you will too if you join us. Good luck with that." She smiled breezily and went back to her laptop.

"It's true, you know," John said, grimly. "I won't pretend otherwise. This job will take over your life, and if it doesn't take over your life, we'll fire you and take on someone who's more dedicated."

"I've worked at start-ups before."

"Not at this one, you haven't," John replied. "Ah, and here's Abhi."

"Morning, Boss," he said, looming in the doorway with a cup of coffee in each hand. The staff at Starbucks had written "Abby" on one of the cups. He kept this for himself and placed the other one in front of Flick. "They never spell my name right," he complained, turning to look at John. "How are you today?"

"Pretty good. This is Dan. He's applying for the developer role. Think you can work with him?"

"You like music, Dan?"

"Of course," I replied.

"Me too," Abhi said. "I can't stand working in silence. Sounds like we're going to be friends."

"Abhi is our back-end developer," John explained.

"That's right, Boss. Can I get you guys a drink?"

"No thanks," John replied. "I'm sure you've got something to work on. Besides, I need a real drink. You coming, Dan?"

"It's eleven AM and I'm being interviewed," I said. "So sure. Why not?"

"That's the spirit. Time doesn't exist in this place. We work when we can, and we drink when we can. Let's go."

***

Flick and Abhi stayed at the "office" while I followed John out the front door, across the road and along a narrow side street. Two minutes later, we were walking through Camden Market, absorbing the dubious sounds and smells of the street dealers who sell grinders and poppers to teenage kids.

We cut through the food stalls with their haunting aromas of fried noodles, strange curries and unpronounceable foreign cuisines and then turned right along the high street. Further down the road, past the neon lights of the Electric Ballroom, we pushed through the crowd outside the station and moved on towards The World's End. Its imposing façade was partly covered by a huge advertisement for the latest iPad. John led the way inside and up to the empty bar. We were served by a tattooed behemoth of a woman who looked like she'd rolled into work after a night at the Ministry of Sound.

"What can I get you?" she asked, without bothering to say hello. Her breath smelled faintly of cigarettes, and she reeked of cheap perfume. Somehow, it was comforting, like when you're walking down the street and a sudden smell sends you back in time.

"Pint of Stella for me, please," said John, pulling a wad of notes from his wallet. "Dan, what's your poison?"

"I'll have a Guinness," I replied. To tell the truth, I needed it. This wasn't what the job ad had led me to expect.

"Guinness, eh? Good man." Beckoning to the barmaid, he muttered something and handed over a couple of bank notes. She came back with a handful of loose change and a packet of dry roasted peanuts. We took our drinks and climbed a red spiral staircase on to a gantry that overlooked the empty interior. We sat down at a table and sipped at our drinks.

"So," said John, trying not to stare at me as I wiped foam from my lip. "You've met the team, or most of them. Peter is away at the moment. He spends a lot of time in Palo Alto. You've seen the office, and not many people see that – believe me. You should have a pretty good idea of our culture, and I presume you know about our product."

"I've got a profile," I replied. "Is that enough?"

"It's a start. Do you have a girlfriend, Dan? A wife? A family?"

"I've not got much of a family. My dad passed away when I was seventeen. Heart attack. Mom remarried. Her and my stepdad are retired now. I don't see them much."

"I'm sorry to hear that, Dan. But it might be for the best. We don't have much time for the living. We're a social network for the dead, after all. What about a partner?"

"Sarah?" I asked. "She's a journalist at TheNextWeb. She works long hours herself, so she knows how it is."

"Does she, now?" mused John, absentmindedly. He sipped from his pint, smacked his lips, opened up the peanuts and continued. "I wonder. This job will kill your social life, and many a start-up has ruined a marriage or a long-term relationship. I'm warning you, Dan, because it's only fair. It takes a big commitment to join this company, and I need you to be aware of what you're getting yourself into before you take the job. What kind of salary are you expecting?"

"Thirty thousand plus," I said, taken aback by the question. "But I'm flexible, really. I'm freelancing at the moment, so any fixed wage is an advantage."

"I'm going to tell you straight, Dan. We can't afford that. If we could, we'd move out of this shithole of an office. We can make a deal, though. We pay all of our employees in stock, at least partially. Peter and I live on our savings. We both sold earlier start-ups. He made more than I did, but I'm not jealous. I have enough to pay the bills. Everything else is just a number on a balance sheet. The rest of the team is paid partly in stock and partly with a salary. It might have some tax benefits as well, but you'll have to talk to Peter about that. You're probably looking at twenty-five thousand pounds plus five thousand pounds of stock per annum, starting after you pass your probation."

"That could work," I said, cautiously. "Does that mean that the job's mine if I want it?"

"Perhaps. I'm going to call you in twenty-four hours. You'll know it's me. Until then, I want you to seriously consider your options. You know how much we're offering. You know our product. You know whether you want to revolutionise the way we look at our digital afterlives. If you decide you want the job, then we'll discuss it. But I'm warning you: once you join us, there's no turning back."

"What is this?" I asked. "Yahoo?"

"Not quite." John picked up his remaining half-pint and downed it in one – all at half eleven on a Monday morning. "Listen, Dan, I've got to go. I'm the only one on the front end at the moment, and we're having teething problems with our new beta. In all seriousness, I hope you'll join us. When you lift up the bonnet, it's a mess. I'm more of a businessman than a programmer, and we need someone who can tidy the code up. This is also your chance to make a difference, to have an impact on a service that's going to change the world. Are you going to spend the rest of your life writing copy for crappy clients? Or do you want to come with us while we disrupt seven shades of shit out of Silicon Valley?"

For the next twenty minutes, John took me through what my role would be, and what I'd be doing on a day-to-day basis. He talked about financials and investments, and how Former.ly had enough venture capital to keep on growing. He talked about variables, and Photoshop, and how I'd be working with Kerry to bring his ideas to life. He talked about users, and how they're the lifeblood of the site, and how he and Peter planned to make money from them and share it out across the rest of the company.

And then, as abruptly as he'd invited me to the pub in the first place, he walked out and left me with half a pint of Guinness and the rest of the peanuts. I did what any sane person would do and started playing Angry Birds while picking at the open bag in front of me. When I finished my first pint, I ordered another.

***

Sarah wasn't in when I got home, so I booted up my machine and sat down in front of it to work on my journal and to play with some code. Technically, I'm unemployed (at least, that's what the taxman thinks), but I do some freelance work on the side as both a writer and a programmer. It's a good life if you love language. It doesn't matter to me whether I'm writing in English, French or

JavaScript.

I'd been tucked away for a couple of hours, tapping away at the keyboard, when I felt a gentle rush of air as the front door opened and closed. There was a jingle of keys as Sarah threw them on to the coffee table, and she entered the study soon afterwards. She dropped a used copy of *The Metro* on to my desk.

"How did it go?" she asked. I kissed her, and she sat down on a beanbag beside me.

"It went well," I said. "Or at least, I think it did. There's a lot for me to think about. It sounds good, but there's got to be a catch. There always is. And I could do it. They need me more than I need them, and they know it."

"Well," Sarah replied, "I'll love and support you no matter what you do."

"You say that now. But have you really thought it through? This could change both of our lives, for better or for worse. It's kind of like betting everything on red and hoping that it pays off. What if it doesn't?"

"I know," she said. "But sometimes you've got to take a chance. Maybe this is one of those times."

"Maybe. I'll think about it."

"You do that," she said, kissing me on the forehead and straightening my tie.

"I will," I promised. "And I think I already know what to do. Now get out of my office. This code won't debug itself."

"Charming. I'll see myself out." To be honest, I was glad to see the back of her. It had been a long, long day.

CHAPTER TWO

TALK ABOUT HANGOVERS. I hadn't hit the town like that since I was a student. It was one of those rare nights when everyone was out in force, and yet no one bitched, argued or otherwise subverted the happy atmosphere.

It was a good night. Sarah got wasted and threw up in the toilet and then spent the taxi ride home telling me how she was proud of me and how she would cover me in her column if I gave her inside information. I hadn't even been offered the job yet! I was expecting John to call me that day, but I still wasn't sure what to say. I would decide in the same way that I always did. I'd wait until the last possible moment and hope that my brain arrived at a decision.

I felt terrible. I tried a cooked breakfast, a pint of orange juice, two showers and a handful of caffeine pills with a mug of black coffee, but none of it helped. I tried coding, but I couldn't concentrate, and I was pretty sure I'd made some changes when I was drunk. In the end, I just lazed around in my underwear and waited for the call. It was an excruciating wait, but the call finally came.

"Hey, is this Dan?" John's voice was muffled but clearly recognisable. Besides, I already knew it was him. I grew so bored while waiting that I assigned a custom ringtone – dubstep — to make sure that I heard it go off. It almost gave me a heart attack when it finally did.

"Speaking," I replied. "How are you, John?"

"Fine, thanks. Have you had time to think things

through?"

"I have," I lied. Sluggishly, I performed the mental equivalent of a coin toss and arrived at a conclusion. "I'm in. I want to go ahead and take the job if it's still available."

"About that. I think you're right for the part, but I can't finalise your contract until you've met Peter. He's coming back this weekend for a party because we just hit a million members. You free on Friday? We'll be going straight from work, so we can meet you there if you like. We're going to the Purple Turtle. Or you can come for pre-drinks at the office."

"Sounds good," I said. "What time do you want me?"

"We'll be hitting the Turtle at nine, so whenever you can make it. See you on Friday?"

"Of course. I'll be there."

"Good man." With the call over and an aching head, I climbed back into bed. I slept all day and woke up just as Sarah got home in the evening.

***

"Did you know that there's a Wikipedia page for Former.ly?" Sarah asked. That was where the two of us were opposites. She was awake and alert in the morning without so much as a coffee, while I rarely even checked my e-mails until the early afternoon. I grunted a half-hearted response.

"Don't worry. It doesn't say anything bad," she continued. "In fact, they seem to have a pretty good reputation as far as I can tell. No real press coverage, but I can change that. I'll put you in touch with a few people."

"I'll introduce you to Flick," I replied. "She's in charge of PR. She seemed nice enough, and she'll be better at schmoozing than I am. I mean, it's her job. My job is to focus on the code, and sometimes just doing that is a struggle."

"I can't wait," she said. "Listen, I've got to go. Some of us have got a job to go to."

"And I will too, soon. Have a great day, babe."

It wasn't until after she left that I realised I'd forgotten to mention the party. Still, I messaged her on Skype and she didn't seem bothered, so I showered and suited up before starting work in my study. It was just the usual – a couple of bug fixes, a request for a quote and a few nagging e-mails to clients who still owed me money.

Most of my clients are friends and family members. They're more likely to give you a shot. As long as they pay up front, you're unlikely to run into problems. Besides, it stops you from wasting time by pitching for work that you're never going to get. I needed to get back to a regular pay cheque, though. My bank account was empty, my overdraft was maxed out, and my credit rating was so bad that I couldn't take out a contract on a mobile phone.

And that was part of the problem. I tapped away at my journal when I should have been writing lines of code or working on headlines that are good enough to convince search engines to index crappy websites that no one's going to buy from. But every great creator kept a journal, and building a website is no different to writing a novel or launching a start-up. A coder is like a singer, and a singer is like an actor. They go out onstage or into the studio and have to pour their hearts out all over again. They have to find the exact emotion that they had in mind when they first put pen to paper. A coder is an artist or a poet, making something beautiful from nothing. That's what I think, anyway.

***

I met the team at the Purple Turtle. Friday was club

night, which no one had bothered to tell me, but luckily I overdressed and so they let me in. After I put down a fiver at the door and had my hand stamped, I spotted Flick and made my way over to her as she swapped a ten-pound note for some change and a White Russian. Abhi stood beside her, sipping at a pint of Cobra. I tried to elbow my way through the crowd, but it was more packed than I'd ever seen it, and I'd seen it filled with both slick city types on pills and sweaty moshers with long hair and leather jackets. Yeah, it was that kind of place.

I settled in for a long wait for an overpriced Guinness. It felt like I'd spent half of my life waiting in queues in dives like this. Either way, I got my Guinness and fought my way through the punters to where the team was gathered around a pair of glowing purple stools, the kind you always seem to get in places where it costs £8.50 for a double gin and tonic. John and Abhi were deep in conversation about the latest problem to plague the front end. Flick sipped at her cocktail nervously, trying vaguely to understand what they were talking about. When she saw me, her eyes lit up like lighthouses when the boats came home.

"Hey, newbie!" she shouted, leaning in so I could hear her above the drum 'n' bass which boomed out from behind the decks. Times had changed since I was a kid. Too late for grunge and Britpop and far too early for emo, my generation had to put up with Shania Twain on the radio, boy bands in pubs and shit techno in clubs. Now, we were all grown up, and we were making the music. Was it any wonder that popular music was at its basest and most cringeworthy nadir in living memory?

Flick was far too drunk to follow my thought process, but she must've noticed me zoning out. "You high?" she asked. "Or just shy?"

"A bit of both," I replied. She just stared at me with

those inscrutable, heavy-lidded eyes of hers. I'd noticed them before and I noticed them now, almost too big for her face and framed with a thin line of Cleopatra-like black eyeliner. I wondered what they looked like first thing in the morning, and I immediately began to blush.

"Oh yeah?" she said. "You don't seem shy to me."

"Well," I replied, "I'm pretty good at pretending to be normal." Someone had joined Abhi and John, and I could just make out the back of his head over Flick's shoulder. She noticed that my eyes had wandered and she turned around too, clutching my arm for support. Abhi was the only one left on the stools; the rest had been occupied by a bunch of skinheads on a stag night. The newcomer was standing to his right, engaging John in an animated conversation.

I turned back to look at Flick. "Who's that?" I asked.

"Oh, him," she replied, rolling her eyes. "That's Peter, the other founder. He's a bit of a bastard."

"I think he knows we're talking about him," I said. "He's coming over."

"He's still a bastard." If he didn't hear her the first time, he heard her then. There was a break in the music, and I was shifting position to shake his hand as she shouted it. Then, the bass dropped, and with a sound like two cars being hit by a freight train, the music drowned everything out. Peter and I were caught in some sort of temporal anomaly, unable to break contact or to stop shaking hands until the bass returned to an acceptable level and we could hear each other.

"Hello, mate," he cried, cupping his short, stubby hands around my ears and shouting so loud that I heard echoes of his voice in the morning. "I'm Peter. You must be Dan. Nice to meet you."

"Likewise! How was Palo Alto?"

"Hot. I didn't get out much, though. There's a certain

irony in what I do. Follow me."

Obediently, I took my drink and followed him as he skulked through the crowd, stocky and determined and ready to barge into the backs of people if they didn't move when he asked them to. He led the way outside, lit a cigarette and shepherded me into a space between two groups of trendies.

"Now," he said, "you're probably wondering why I brought you out here."

"I figured you wanted a cigarette," I said.

"Well, there is that. Do you smoke, Dan?"

"No, sir," I replied. "I haven't smoked since I was seventeen, not properly. But I'll take the odd cigarette when I'm drunk."

"Well, we'll work on that tonight." He leaned in closer and put his smoke-free arm around me. "Dan, let me get straight to the point," he said. "You've met the rest of the team, if only briefly, and they're already convinced you're the man for the job. Abhi is keen, as is John. He's a lousy developer and he knows it. You can do stuff he could never do. He wants to learn from you."

"I hope I don't disappoint," I said. I meant it too. By now, my mind was made up. Opportunities don't come around often, and if we end up as one of the 40 percent of start-ups that fail then at least we tried.

"I don't think you'll disappoint anyone, Dan. Think you're ready to change the world?"

"If I'm not, then I'll die trying," I laughed. "Does this mean I'm in?"

"You're keen and I like that, but you're not in just yet. We'll see how you get on tonight. This is your second interview, Dan. Don't fuck it up. Let us see your fun side. We'll start with a Jägerbomb."

"Sounds like my kind of interview," I replied. Peter

stubbed out his cigarette and led the way back inside and over to the rest of the team, who'd managed to find a table. We sat down just as Flick staggered over with a tray of drinks: a fresh pint for each of the boys, another cocktail for herself, and a round of Jägerbombs in dirty glasses."

"You read my mind," shouted Peter, grabbing her by the elbow once the shots were on the table. "Give mine to the newbie."

"What are you talking about?" she giggled. "They're all for him. He's got some catching up to do."

***

Much, much later, Flick was all over me on the dance floor. It was half-embarrassing, half-flattering. I never got much attention from the ladies. It came with the territory. Developers were only attractive to female developers, unless they made plenty of money. Still, I didn't let the booze get the better of me. Flick was wasted, and I had a woman waiting for me when I got home.

Perhaps that was because of what Peter said. Earlier in the evening when I bumped into him in the gents, he'd given me a warning. "Watch out for Flick," he'd said. "She always gets drunk at these things. She's worse than any of the guys. She tries to outdrink us, succeeds for a couple of hours, and then we all catch up and overtake her when she's hammered."

"I'll bear that in mind," I replied. That was two hours ago. If she was close to the edge then, she was well past the point of no return now. She cornered me on the dance floor and started grinding up against me.

"You know," she said, rising above the clamour of the music by brushing her lips against my ear. "I don't live at that slum with the rest of the guys. How do you feel about coming back to my place?"

She was a good-looking girl, and I was hardly a catch. And I was drunk, sure. I just wasn't drunk enough to cheat on Sarah. It wasn't worth the long nights of endless arguments or the dawning realisation that I just didn't love her anymore. Besides, this was still technically a job interview, and I'd be damned if I'd sleep with someone to get a job when my brains alone should have been enough.

"I'm sorry, Flick," I replied. "I can't. I've got a girlfriend." She laughed.

"You've got a girlfriend?" she said. "Well, that won't last for long." Suddenly and unexpectedly, she burst into tears, right there on the dance floor. The rest of the team had disappeared, probably to the bar or to the smoking area, so I put my arm around her shoulder and guided her to a nearby booth where we sat down for a moment of privacy.

"What's wrong?" I asked, placing my hand on her arm. She composed herself hurriedly, did her best to fix her make-up with the help of a compact mirror, and then brushed her hair out of her face to reply to me.

"Oh nothing," she murmured, half to herself. "I just get lonely sometimes. This job really does kill your social life. My ex left me six weeks after I started, and I don't have much of a family. Last I heard, Dad's living in Gibraltar in early retirement with the insurance money. I never saw a penny. Mum died when I was fifteen. She was only thirty-three. Epilepsy, they said. She'd never shown symptoms before. Then, she had a seizure in her sleep. She never woke up." Flick smiled sadly for the first time since the dance floor.

"I'm sorry to hear that," I said, softly.

"It's not your fault, and I'm sorry for the state I'm in. It happens, you know? It just makes you think. If I die at the same age, I'm two-thirds of the way through my life. It'd drive anyone to drink."

"She'd be proud of you," I told her, despite the evidence to the contrary. "Besides, believe it or not, I know how you feel. My dad died when I was seventeen. A heart attack. We were never close, and so it didn't mess me up like it could have, but people were never the same to me afterwards. I was always 'that kid with the dead dad.' I don't really like to talk about it. Even Sarah doesn't know the whole truth."

"Is that your girlfriend?" Flick asked. "She's a lucky girl, and I'm flattered. Thanks, Dan. I feel better. You're a good friend. I've only met you twice, but I can tell. Now, I hate to put a downer on things, but I'm going home. Tell the boys for me, will you?"

***

It turned out that the rest of the team had already left, leaving me drunk in the city with just enough money to get home. I could've killed for cheesy chips, but instead I found myself catching a taxi home with a rumbling stomach. I managed to open the door to the flat after my third attempt.

I was expecting Sarah to be asleep, but she was watching TV in her dressing gown when I returned. She turned it off with a flick of the remote and stood up as I stumbled into the living room. Her hazel eyes seethed with repressed fury as she ran her hands nervously through her elven hair.

"Where the hell have you been?" she asked. Her voice rang with a brutal steel edge, a warning of things to come. "Do you have any idea what time it is? I've been worried sick."

"About four-ish?" I hazarded.

"It's half past five in the morning, Dan. I've been calling you all evening. Have you checked your voicemail? Did you get my texts?"

"What is this, the Spanish Inquisition? I ran out of battery. I'm sorry. Cool off. I'm back now. I just want to go to bed."

"I didn't get any sleep," she chided. "So why should you? I'm supposed to get up in an hour, and you're just rolling through the door."

"I'm sorry," I said, slouching towards her and wrapping my arms resentfully around her shoulders. She smiled for a second, but then her smile froze.

"What the hell is this?" she screeched. "And don't give me any of your bullshit. You stink of perfume! You smell like another woman! Where the hell have you been?"

"I've been at the goddamn Purple Turtle," I growled, drunken anger rising in my chest. "With the guys from Former.ly. My second interview, I'll have you know. The drunker I was, the more likely I was to get the job. You should be proud of me!"

"Proud?" she howled, glaring at me through a faint fog of tears. In one swift and unexpected movement, she swept her arm across the table and sent my laptop crashing to the floor. "Then why do you smell like some slag's cheap perfume?"

"That? That's probably Flick. I told you about her, right?"

"Yeah," she sobbed. "You did." With a rage that I've seen too often, Sarah swept up her car keys and stormed out of the flat, still in her dressing gown.

I was too drunk to care. I can be an asshole like that, and she should know that by now. The harsh truth of it was that she was getting angry over nothing. Even though I could see why she'd be suspicious, she didn't give me a chance to explain myself. This wasn't the movies, and I wasn't about to chase her. After all, it was, as she'd pointed out, half past five in the morning. My bed was calling.

CHAPTER THREE

I DIDN'T SPEAK to Sarah for four days after that. She stayed away from the flat and blanked me on Facebook and Twitter. She didn't reply to my two tentative e-mails nor to my calls or my texts, so I finally got the message and left her to it. It wasn't the first time that this had happened. Sarah had always been unpredictable, ever since university when she'd missed a semester to go travelling in India and ended up working in an Australian dive bar.

She came back from Australia with her tail between her legs and then promptly went missing again. This time, she was picked up by the police, stumbling drunkenly along a dual carriageway at four o'clock in the morning. That was when her doctor suggested counselling, but she didn't go for it. Instead, she took the mood stabilisers he offered her and tried to get on with her life. She didn't like to talk about it, but I'd been with her for long enough to know that sometimes she liked to do things that didn't make sense to anyone else. It was one of the reasons why I fell in love with her, but after a while, it stopped being cute and started to get on my nerves.

When she finally returned my calls, I found out that she was staying at her mother's, which didn't surprise me. I barely saw my family, but she saw hers all the time. She was just a spoilt little kid at heart, and it bugged me. I'd had to make my own way ever since Dad died, and she took stuff for granted that I'd never been lucky enough to experience.

She called me, eventually, to apologise. She said she'd been unreasonable and that there might have been a good explanation. As I was only too happy to tell her, there was.

"Oh," she replied. "I was under the impression that I was single. Still, no real harm done." And that was that. She wouldn't say any more on the subject. She just threw out a line like that as if it was nothing, leaving me to try to figure out what she meant. Had she slept with someone else? And, despite what she said, did she still think I hooked up with Flick? Did it even matter?

John called me while I was sitting in Starbucks, drinking a latte and working on the latest problem to present itself.

"I've got good news for you," he said, getting straight to the point. I was glad for the lack of small talk. I hate talking on the phone, especially in public. "I've just got off a call with Peter, and we've come to an agreement. Long story short, you're in."

"Oh, that's fantastic news!" I was so surprised that I almost spilled my coffee on the keyboard. "When do I start?"

"As soon as you can. Tomorrow, if you can make it." I started to laugh and then realised he was serious. I had some freelance obligations to finish off, but I figured I could do those in the evenings. I told him I could start right away.

"Good!" he exclaimed. "Then I'll see you tomorrow. Bring a packed lunch. We're throwing you in at the deep end, and you won't have time to go to the pub every day. We save that for Fridays as a rule."

At the time, it didn't really sink in. I just ended the call and turned back to the laptop to close a few tags and test my script before saving, shutting down and walking back to the flat.

It wasn't until the evening that I celebrated, and boy, did I celebrate.

***

So that was how I came to start my new job on four hours of sleep, nursing a hangover with a five o'clock shadow. Still, I got there at nine on the dot and was greeted by John, the young founder, who was wearing a pair of white Reebok Classics and a fluffy pink dressing gown, holding a steaming cup of coffee to ward off the autumnal chill.

"You're early," he said, stepping aside so I could enter the office. It looked cleaner than before, suspiciously so.

"You said to be here at nine," I reminded him, pointing at the time on my iPhone.

"Yeah," John said, shrugging. "But I'm used to people running an hour late. We usually start around ten, and we finish when we're finished. Come on in, though." I stepped over the threshold and debated whether to take my shoes off. Was I a guest, or did I "live" there now? In the end, I followed John's lead and left them on, then walked into the living room after a moment's hesitation.

"What's with the dressing gown?" I asked.

John shrugged. "I have bigger things on my mind than the clothes I wear," he replied.

"I see," I said. "And what about the sudden cleanliness? Last time I came in here, it looked like the big bad wolf had been trying to blow the house down."

John laughed, pausing slightly before replying. "We might be coming into some money," he explained, carefully. "That's why we're hiring you. We decided to get a cleaner too. God knows, this place needs a good scrubbing."

"It looks like someone lives here," I told him.

"They do," he replied. "I live here, and so does Kerry. Peter does too when he's around. He's got a mattress in the boardroom, which happens to look suspiciously like a living room. At times, you'll feel like you live here too."

"I'll make myself at home, then. Where do you want me?"

"Just sit yourself down there," he said, directing me to a low sofa opposite a TV set. I recognised it as the sofa where Kerry had lain comatose at the start of my first interview. It was vacant now, but it smelled like a locker room and sank down beneath me when I sat on it. Unperturbed, I logged on to the wireless with a password that Peter shouted through from the kitchen. I nodded at Kerry as he filtered into the living room to get started on the morning's work. From the hallway, I heard the muffled sound of someone letting themselves in through the front door. Abhi appeared shortly afterwards.

"Morning, Dan," he said, shaking my hand and pulling up beside me on the sofa. "I'm glad you're here. We need you. Here, take this." He handed me a yellow Post-it Note which was covered in a woman's tidy, spidery handwriting. "It's your login. Get online, check your e-mails and get to work. You should have a couple dozen of low-priority jobs to be getting on with. We've been forwarding stuff over ever since we knew you were joining us. Let me know if you need help getting onto the server. Flick says she wrote everything down, but between you and me, she wouldn't know a DNS from an ISP."

"Thanks," I replied, tapping away at my keyboard. "Looks like I'm in. Christ, one hundred and ninety-two unread e-mails. Not bad for my first day."

"Sounds about right," Abhi replied. "We assigned some bug fixes to get you started. If you need me, come get me. I'll be in the bedroom."

"Like hell you will," shouted Peter, who still clattering away in the kitchen. "I've booked it today, Abhi.

Sit your ass back down beside the newbie and show him the ropes. Someone has to."

"Sure thing, Boss," he murmured.

"What's the deal with the bedroom?" I asked.

"We don't have private rooms, see," Abhi explained, muttering in a low, rebellious overtone. "The bedroom is the next best thing. It's easier to work in there. You don't have to put up with people breathing down your neck for scrappy favours that distract you from the database."

I said nothing. I was busy working through a flood of e mails, mostly for Viagra and dubious dating sites. Abhi didn't care. He just booted up a machine of his own and started coding. I felt like I knew him already. He seemed like a natural-born pessimist, a complainer who never did anything to change things. I planned to change that.

***

Throughout the morning, we worked in silos, with each of us doing our own thing while Abhi streamed hip-hop from his iPhone. Every time I had a question, I only got half an answer, and it didn't take me long to realise I was in over my head. Something strange was going on. I could sense it.

John wanted me to work on isolated chunks of code, slotting variables into place in a front-end design that Kerry had sent over. They had a strange way of working, and it bothered me. John and Peter came up with the designs and functionality and then filtered them down in a collection of meta-scripts, cryptic sketches and hand-drawn diagrams. Kerry created the visuals, Abhi built the database and coded the PHP, and I brought the two together, slotting variables into place like a paint-by-numbers. It was crazy, really. Everything took twice as long, and there was no need for it. In fact, I confronted John about it in the kitchen, when the others were out of earshot.

"So what gives?" I asked. "Abhi won't even talk about it. He just says it's the way things have always been done."

"Abhi said that, did he? I wonder. I presume you're talking about our unique way of working."

"Damn right," I replied, feeling flustered. I didn't want to lose the gig, but I already knew that they needed me. When I lifted up the bonnet, it was a mess, just like John had told me. I figured I could afford to ask a few questions. "How come we work in silos? You know damn well that we could work more efficiently if you didn't try to hide the way the site works."

"We have our reasons," he replied, cautiously. "And you'd do well to remember your place. You're still on probation, remember. But as you asked, I'll tell you. We've had leaks before, and you can't be too careful. It's just the way that we work. Don't ask questions. Just stick at it, and you'll see the full source code once we trust you."

"I see," I said. "So that's how it is. I'll see what I can do. You'd better start trusting me soon, though. It's a mess in there."

"Tell me about it," he replied. And that was that. I guessed it was something I'd have to learn to live with. Still, once I knew where I stood, Abhi opened up and started to speak to me. He didn't tell me anything I couldn't have found out elsewhere, though.

The site itself was pretty simple, even if it was often difficult to tell what was happening when you looked at the source code. Once you signed up to the site, you were able to post status updates, photos and videos, which remained visible only to the user until their death. You could even upload files and customise your privacy settings. Then, after your death, your cache of content was released into the wild.

When I joined, the company had just registered their five

hundredth death, and so the site was still in its infancy. I wasn't sure, but I presumed that I was there to work on a bunch of new features, like following functionality and virtual gravestones. For now, though, I was stuck working on bug fixes. John's coding was atrocious. I'd never seen anything like it. There was no documentation, and all of the variables were code-named as per his bizarre requirements. I had my work cut out for me.

The biggest mystery was how we were able to tell whether someone was dead or not. I asked John about it, but he kept schtum.

"Can't tell you that," he replied, looking stern and authoritative, despite his fluffy dressing gown. "If I told you, I'd have to kill you. Just let me worry about that. For now, all you need to know is that we know, at least for most of the major countries and several of the smaller ones. In some regions, friends and family members have to contact us with a death certificate, and Flick processes them manually. It's a temporary solution and it isn't scalable, so that's one of the things I'll be working on now that we've taken you on and freed up some of my time."

"I see," I said. "Anything I can help with?"

"No. You shouldn't even know about it. Forget I mentioned it." Of course, I didn't. Instead, I filed the information away in case it came in useful at a later date. I didn't understand the need for secrecy; I've always preferred an open organisation. Still, a job was a job.

And so I got straight back to work. John and Peter had me working with Flick to deploy a survey on the site. The idea was to get feedback from our users so that we could tailor the site to suit their needs. There was even whispered talk of deploying a new language pack. I didn't know it at the time, but Former.ly's surveys would become one of our selling points, like Google's Doodles or sexting on Snapchat.

The users loved it.

I was indifferent. It was a challenge and one that needed to be completed. But first, there were bug fixes to deal with.

***

It was a long, fulfilling first day. John insisted that all of the fixes needed to be on the staging site before I left, so he could review them and push them live in the middle of the night when traffic was at its lowest.

"Sleep with your phone beside you," he said, as I shut down my laptop, drained my coffee and prepared to drive home. "You never know when you'll be needed."

"Do you wake your employees often?"

"Maybe once a month if you're lucky and you don't fuck up. You'll hear from me on weekends too. I expect you to check your e-mails and to work remotely when required."

"That's not going to sit well with Sarah," I told him. "But who cares? I'm in. I'll see you tomorrow."

"Thanks, Dan."

Flick told me later that you would be more likely to hear the Pope say "fuck" than to hear John say "thanks," so I guess I made a good first impression. I just hoped that I could keep up the good work. I wanted them to keep me on. Not because I needed the job or for the thrill of working at a start-up, but because the secretive code behind the site and John's erratic behaviour had set off my spider senses. Something strange was going on; I intended to find out what it was.

CHAPTER FOUR

IT WAS TWO WEEKS later, and London was covered by a blanket of fine mist that seemed to soak through clothes, skin and bones. It was horrible. On days like those, I found it hard to get out of bed until the pathetic plug-in heater kicked in and warmed the room up. I woke with a sense of deep, dark foreboding. My workload had grown exponentially, and I'd already stayed late three times that week, once until eleven PM.

My fears turned out to be grounded. John had rolled back a bunch of fixes, so I effectively had to finish three days of work in one. The guys went to the pub at lunchtime, but I stayed behind and powered through, though I did share a bottle of wine with Flick, who was also staying in the office. The lead singer of an obscure K-pop band collapsed and died on stage the night before, launching his profile amidst a wave of publicity. Tributes from his fans and fellow musicians soon stated pouring in, and for 24-hours or so we were the hottest site on the internet. It was just the sort of story that went down well with the media.

"In our case," she told me, "there really is no such thing as bad publicity. Death always puts a negative spin on an article. We have to accept that and move on. Besides, journalists love death. Nothing sells papers like a tragedy. *The Sun* has already agreed to run with it."

"Yeah? Whose soul did you sell to place that?"

"No one's," she laughed. "I just spent the morning on

Twitter and waited for nature to take its course. Nowadays, anyone has a shot at greatness as long as they have a Twitter account and a story to tell."

"And you have both."

"Of course," she replied. "Most people do. They just don't always realise it." Her phone rang out from the table and she excused herself to answer it. By the time that she put the phone down, I was balls deep in John's messy source code. We both worked on in silence until the rest of the team made their inebriated return.

***

I didn't get home until quarter to one in the morning. It was a long day, and I had more amends to make over the weekend. My schedule was further complicated by the fact that the chunk of code I was working on was so messed up that it was easier for me to track down the original diagram and to recode the whole thing from scratch. Who knew a search bar could cause such problems?

When I got home, Sarah was sitting cross-legged on the sofa with a glass of wine in one hand and the TV remote in the other. She hit the mute button as I walked in and then unexpectedly called me a bastard.

"How dare you just stroll in as though nothing is wrong?" she demanded. "They're working you too hard. Can't you see that? They're going to drive you into the ground, and I'm going to have to sit here and watch them do it."

"I'm sorry," I replied, a little annoyed because I hadn't done anything wrong. Did she think that I wanted to work late on a Friday, surrounded by the funk of fully grown men who rarely showered? "It's my own fault. I spent the day fixing some mistakes that I made."

"Yeah? And what did you spend the night doing, huh? You've been gone for nearly eighteen hours. Have you been working the whole time?"

"For most of it," I replied, sheepishly avoiding her gaze. "We ordered a pizza, and so we stopped for a while to eat it. Apart from that, we worked throughout the day. Flick and I even stayed through lunch while the rest of the team was at the pub."

"Bullshit, Dan," she snapped. "This is like your fling with Anna all over again."

"That was years ago. Besides, we were on a break."

"Yeah? Well, let's hope you're ready for another one. I'm not sharing you with anyone, Dan. Don't you think it's strange that you spend more time in her company than in mine?"

"Not really," I replied. "We work together. I'd say that's pretty normal."

"You know what I mean. You're spending twelve hours a day at the office and by the time you get home, you're ready to go to bed. What does that say about our relationship? What does that say about you?"

"It'll get better," I promised. "And it'll be worth it. Besides, you can talk. What about all the times you jetted off to France for Le Web or to the States for Disrupt? You just left me here with no money, no food and a mountain of work to get through. All this shit didn't matter then, did it? And what about when I took the job? You knew what I was getting into, and you said you were cool with it. What happened to being cool?"

"How dare you?" she scowled. "There's a difference between being supportive and being a doormat. Besides, maybe I was wrong. At first, I thought it would be good for us. But it's not. It's not good at all. I'm unhappy, Dan, and I have been since you took the job. Is this really what you want? 'Cause you're on thin ice, Dan. You've got some thinking to do. You can sleep on the sofa tonight."

***

When I returned to the office on Monday, I was surprised to see Peter wearing a pair of chinos, a Washington State University hoodie and a DKNY baseball cap. He was in the kitchen, brewing a pot of coffee. I guess the founders had more pressing concerns than fashion, but there was such a thing as common sense. He looked like he'd been involved in an explosion at a launderette.

"Dan," he said. "Good to see you, buddy. How are you settling in?"

"It's already a second home," I replied. "What brings you here?"

"I just got back from Palo Alto. I've been sweet-talking a few old contacts to see what I can get out of them. Servers, space, support – a bit of money would be nice too."

"Abhi said we keep the servers in the loft," I said. "Is that true?"

"Abhi said that? Well, he told you the truth, although he should've kept his mouth shut."

"Why do you keep the servers in the loft?" I asked.

"John and I like to be in control," Peter said, carefully. "We want the servers to be somewhere that no one else has access to. There are some evil people in this world, Dan. You've got to be on your guard at all times."

"But the loft? I mean, really? What about the Cloud? Why bother with your own set of servers when you could use a third-party provider?"

"It's the best place for them," Peter said. "There's always someone here, and John and I are the only people with access. We've got a good enough connection, good enough for now at least. If we can avoid sharing data with a third party, then we'll do so. Why hire space on someone else's servers when you could build your own? Besides, we've got the best sysadmin in the city."

"Who's that, then?"

"Me," he replied, swelling with pride and self-satisfaction. I let it go at that.

Like John, Peter preferred to work alone to avoid the inevitable distractions caused by sitting in a room with Flick and Kerry for hours on end. While John worked from the bedroom, Peter sat amongst the servers in the loft and left the rest of us to fight it out for space in the living room. We were tapping happily away at our keyboards when Flick came off the phone, placed her mobile on the desk beside her and began to laugh.

"I did it," she giggled. "I finally fucking did it." She laughed again, looked back at her screen and then sighed. "Gentlemen, I hope you're ready for this 'cause traffic's about to go through the roof."

"Why?" I asked her. "What did you do?"

"Oh, just my little stroke of genius. Paid placements. It's the way forward."

"You mean like adverts?"

"No," she replied. "I mean like taking advantage of idiots on Facebook. I've just been talking to a guy in the Philippines who runs a Christian Facebook page so he can sell ad space. For a couple of hundred quid, he'll include our link in the description of his next post."

"Yeah?" Kerry said. "And what kind of stuff does he post?"

"You know, the usual. Bible quotes, 'one like equals one prayer,' that sort of shit."

"I know the type," Kerry told her, vaguely. "You get a lot of those back home in the States. But I never knew there was money in it. How many followers does he have?"

"Eight hundred thousand, give or take a couple of hundred," Flick said. "His last link got three hundred and seventy-five thousand clicks in two days."

"Nice," I replied. "That's a decent chunk of traffic. Shame it's not really relevant."

"Not really relevant?" Flick laughed. "Plugging Former.ly to religious zealots is as relevant as you can get. We need to reach a large crowd of gullible people who'll believe anything we tell them. Where better to look than organised religion? Besides, they love life after death, and that's what our site is all about."

"Touché," I replied. "And when's the placement going live?"

Flick refreshed her Facebook feed and scowled. "Any second now," she said. "I'd better go and warn Peter. Let's hope the servers are up to scratch."

***

The post went live later that afternoon, and the servers were immediately hit by a surge of traffic that threatened to take us offline. Peter's happy mood rapidly deteriorated as the dilapidated infrastructure started to crumble. I had to draft Flick in to help me to prioritise the bug reports that were slowly trickling in. John, meanwhile, was sent out with the company credit card to buy some new equipment to prop the system up.

Traffic peaked about an hour after the link first went out and then calmed down and built back up to a second, higher peak six hours later. Flick said that the post was getting a second wind, as people shared the original shares. Either way, we weren't complaining. We were signing up a dozen new members a minute – a higher registration rate than ever before.

"Forget about the servers," Peter said, when the team sat down for a celebratory cup of coffee after the initial onslaught was over. "What about the database?"

To tell the truth, I had worries of my own. It was like running a Super Bowl advert for a local diner. People were coming in from all over the world, and we struggled to meet the demand. In the first six hours, we received reports of a half dozen major security flaws, as well as more than a hundred minor glitches that we hadn't picked up on before. One guy from Singapore was only a couple of steps away from getting into the back end, which is never good.

Of course, I got home later than I wanted to, and I got the feeling that Sarah wasn't happy. The flat was mysteriously empty, and when I tried to call her, it went straight to voicemail. I left a message at the tone.

"Hey babe, it's me. I'm guessing you're mad at me again, huh? Well, whatever. I'm home now. I guess I'll see you in the morning."

CHAPTER FIVE

IT WAS A COLD, cold Thursday at the start of December when I first put my foot in it. Until then, I'd kept my nose clean and worked hard, and the hard work had paid off. John had given me access to longer sections of code, although I couldn't make sense of most of it. The workload had calmed down too. I wasn't freelancing at the weekend, and I was usually home by eight during the week.

Things with Sarah had calmed down too. Oh, sure, we still didn't see eye to eye on things, but she was happy to be able to spend some time with me, and I did my best to make her feel like a kid again, even if I was just cuddling up next to her while she watched *Grey's Anatomy*. For the first time in a couple of months, she responded, and we came together like opposite ends of a magnet. Life was pretty sweet.

That is, it was pretty sweet until that fateful morning when I walked in on a private meeting between John and Peter. The two founders were talking together in a low monotone. Whatever they were talking about looked serious. Peter's usual good-natured smile had been replaced by a serpentine grin, and John never looked too happy at the best of times. Now, he looked positively demonic, and that was before he saw me.

I only overheard odd words – some talk about "source codes," "death" and "overload." They might as well have been talking about a role-playing game for all the sense it made to me. They didn't seem too happy when they saw me, though.

Peter saw me first, and his eyes narrowed in confusion. They were both standing with their backs to the open door, and I hadn't knocked before I entered. There didn't seem to be much point. Nobody knocked in that house. Everyone just walked around like they lived there, in some cases because they did. When John noticed that he no longer had Peter's full attention, he followed his gaze and then exploded.

"Dan!" he cried, almost propelling himself into the air. "What the hell are you doing here?"

"The internet's gone down again. You said you wanted me to tell you if…"

"To hell with that," he shouted. I took a step backwards without even noticing. "Were you raised in a fucking barn, Dan? Why didn't you knock?"

"We never knock," I reminded him. "That's just the way it is."

"Yeah? Well, maybe we'd better start if you're going to go sneaking around like this. What did you overhear? Tell me!" He took another step closer, and I stepped even further backwards, out into the hallway.

"I didn't hear anything," I protested. "I don't know what you were talking about. But if you want me to go, then I'll go."

"Then go," he snarled. "And don't tell anyone else about this. This conversation never happened."

"You're the boss," I replied, backing slowly further down the hallway. John slammed the door in my face as I retreated, and I heard his muffled voice through the wall as he resumed his conversation. For a guy who was so obsessed with secrecy, he had a pretty loud voice when he let his emotions take over.

I was in for another surprise when I got to the bottom of the stairs. Flick was sitting on the bottom step, grinning expectantly. When she saw my ashen face, she laughed.

"Who's a naughty boy, then?" she asked, pointing back in the direction of the bedroom. "What have you been doing to annoy them?"

"I haven't been doing anything," I told her. "John just flipped. I don't know why."

"He does that," she told me. "Did you walk in on him without knocking?"

"Yeah. He was talking to Peter."

"That'll be it, then," Flick shrugged. "Abhi walked in on him when he was doing the finances once. John went ballistic. He threw a chair across the room."

"I can believe it," I said. "What happened next?"

"Nothing, really. Abhi worked from home for a couple of days and then came in again the following week. Everyone pretended that nothing had happened. You'll get used to it."

***

It was that horrible time of year when Christmas songs were on the radio and everyone started getting into the so-called "spirit." Flick spent the afternoon taking calls in a Santa hat, and Kerry tied tinsel around his tripod. They were working together, filming a festive video to go out to our e-mail list. John had been right when he'd first told me about the American filmmaker's abilities. With the right lighting, he could make the flat shine like a Hollywood studio. He'd already hit a million views with an animation on our YouTube channel. Clever guy!

That day, he was interviewing each of the team members about their friends, their family and their childhood. I was dreading it. I'm not a fan of Christmas. I already had to put up with Sarah rabbiting on about it whenever she was actually talking to me. The last thing I wanted was to hear about it in the office too.

I was looking up intermittently, with my head down and my headphones on, dual-screening with a Google I/O talk on in the background – standard practice. We all have our own ways of surviving in the madhouse. When I next looked up, it was like looking into a scene from a horror film. Flick was sitting on an aluminium stool, illuminated by Kerry's rig and staring into a camera as he interrogated her in front of a green screen. It was fascinating.

"My mother died on Christmas Day," Flick was saying. "After that, we didn't really celebrate. It became one of those things that we just had to get through, you know? But we still spend it together as a family. We visit Mum's grave and feel thankful that no one else has gone."

"I see," said Kerry, moving from the camera to the rig. "What about presents? You must've given gifts, right?"

"Oh yeah," she replied. "Loads of them. They were just crappy gifts that no one ever wanted. One year, I got a cactus, a stationery set and a Gameboy game. I didn't even own a Gameboy. Another year, I got a bike which turned out to be stolen. But you've got to be grateful for whatever you get, I guess."

At that point, I zoned out again to deal with a pair of tricky variables which kept on breaking the headers. When I started paying attention again, Flick had moved on to the subject of Father Christmas. She was more animated now, and Kerry clearly wasn't listening to a word that she was saying.

"I first found out he wasn't real when he got busted. He was some drunk from my dad's local boozer, who played Santa at the fayre. There were some accusations. Then the press got hold of it. After that, I never saw him again."

Kerry switched his camera off and Flick exhaled heavily. The heat from the lights had melted her lipstick, and the sweat had smudged her mascara. She stood stock still, like a widow at a funeral. Then, suddenly, she laughed and walked over to her desk. I watched all this happen in vague bewilderment and then asked her the inevitable question.

"Was that for the public?"

"Of course, it was," Kerry said, as he helped Flick to remove her lapel mic. "We're filming this on John's orders. Flick here agrees with him."

"That's right," she beamed. "Every start-up under the sun is putting out a video. Ours is just a bit more honest. You've got to be brutal to cut through the noise, Dan. You've got to do something so incredibly different that people don't just stop and listen. You've got to grab them by the balls. You've got to make them take notice and start talking. This will just give them something to talk about."

"And was it true?" I asked.

Flick's smile faltered, and her heavy eyelids seemed to darken. "Mostly," she replied.

She didn't say a word for the rest of the afternoon, except for when she answered the phone to a salesman and told him to fuck off. After she'd washed her face and reapplied her make-up, she looked as stunning and as strong as ever, but there was something in her eyes that only I could see. Remorse, perhaps.

***

That evening, I sat at my desk for hours, updating my journal with the latest developments. Sarah and I weren't getting on so well. I suspected her of jealousy, and she suspected me of cheating. No matter how many times I told her that I wasn't sleeping with Flick, she wouldn't believe me.

See, Sarah changed her mind a lot. At first, she'd been indifferent, and maybe even a little excited. She'd even encouraged me to take the job, but once she found out how much work it would take, her mind went into overdrive. Paranoia and jealousy at a ridiculous scale.

These days, she thought I was crazy to have taken the job in the first place. In her little world, the only reason I took it was so that I could try to hook up with Flick. Sarah had never even met her, and maybe that was part of the problem. She'd never really trusted me, and I don't blame her. She had a rough past, filled with dickhead exes and a former lecturer who'd started rubbing her thigh during a one-to-one. Perhaps we weren't the best combination, but when you're lonely, you'll take what you can get. Besides, the rent's cheaper when you split it with someone else.

Even if I liked Flick, I thought she was more interested in Peter. After all, he was charismatic, he was mysterious, and he was never in the country. They say absence makes the heart grow fonder. They were perfect for each other.

I stopped writing for a second to crack open another beer, my fourth of the evening. A cold chill down the back of my neck gave me the feeling that someone was watching me. Sure enough, I turned around to see Sarah standing there seductively, dressed in a sexy black negligee and holding a mug of hot chocolate in one of her hands.

"What are you up to?" she asked. I breathed a silent sigh of relief. She wasn't here to pick a fight.

"Writing in my journal," I told her. "It's been over a week since I caught up with things. Time flies when you're having fun."

"Okay, babe. Just come to bed soon. I'm stressed and in need of affection." She kissed me on the cheek and left me in front of my machine, where I sat in thoughtful silence for five minutes to gather my thoughts. That morning, she wouldn't have given me the time of day.

My journal was going to have to wait. Sometimes, there were more important things to do than to write down everything that happened in the hope that someday it would serve a purpose. I powered down my machine, brushed my teeth in a hurry, spritzed myself with deodorant and made my way into the bedroom.

By the time that I got there, Sarah was already asleep.

***

I was hard at work the following day, trying to develop what seemed to be a rudimentary checkout system, when John entered the cluttered living room and called for silence. Kerry, who was halfway through a box of popcorn chicken, left his computer to render and wandered over. I waited for Flick to finish her phone call and then saved my code and closed my laptop.

"Listen up," John said, rapping his knuckles against a baking tray in an unnecessary attempt to gain our attention. "I've got an announcement to make. We're moving, and we're moving soon – next month, in fact. Peter's been working on it for most of the year, but we wanted to keep it secret – a surprise. We've secured new offices just off Tottenham Court Road. Peter's got some old friends who owe him a favour."

"This is big news," Flick replied. "I'll get out a press release. Where are we getting the money from?"

"I can't tell you that. Let's just say that we've come into some money. We've got a couple of interns joining us too. They want to code, but that's not going to happen. They can earn our trust and work their way up like everyone else.

They'll be joining us in a couple of weeks, working two days a week for the foreseeable future. They'll be working with Flick to begin with, getting the new office sorted out and helping with our marketing."

"Sounds good," I said. "We're going to need some help if we keep on growing."

"They can help me in the studio too," Kerry added, sucking chicken juice from his massive hands. "Three heads are better than one."

"Precisely," replied John, evenly. "Pack up your stuff whenever you get time. If it's not packed into boxes, then it won't get picked up when the van comes round. Flick, I'll send you the details for the new office. Circulate the info and update whatever needs updating. Get business cards and stationery printed too. Peter's sorted out the broadband, but you'll want to get fixed lines put in place and God knows what else. We'll give you a budget to decorate the place too. We're going pro, folks. Let's hope we can rise to the challenge."

CHAPTER SIX

ON THE FOLLOWING SUNDAY, we hit a major milestone – fifty million registrations, as well as our eleven thousandth death. Flick sent me an IM to tell me that she'd been summoned to the brand new office. Even though it was the weekend, she was keen to get things started. Sarah was out of the house and I needed to shift some code, so I said I'd meet Flick there.

Ten minutes after agreeing to meet Flick, I was descending an escalator towards the Central Line with my laptop tucked under my arm because Sarah took my rucksack with her to the gym. I hate the Tube. It's dark and it's dirty and too full of sweaty commuters. Luckily, the commuter crowd disperses over the weekend. When someone's working on their laptop on the Tube on a Sunday, they're either self-employed or they work for a start-up.

I got off the Tube at Tottenham Court Road and felt glad to be back in the sunlight, even though it was bitterly cold. Luckily, the new office wasn't far away. I dodged through the milling crowd past a news booth, cut across the busy road and walked beneath the bridge towards Denmark Street, the only place in the world that makes me want to learn to play the sitar. Former.ly's new office was on a small road to the back of it, on the second floor of a dilapidated old building which was ultra-modern as soon as you stepped over the threshold. It was clean and empty, but there was still a vibe about the place that reminded me of the old "office" in the living room of John and Kerry's flat.

Unsurprisingly, Flick was already there when I arrived. Likewise, John and Abhi were at their desks, but Kerry, Peter and the two new interns were right where they should be, enjoying whatever they did in their free time. Me? I didn't have a life, and I was fine with that. My mind rebelled at stagnation. Give me work! Give me problems! Give me a server on a Saturday and I was like a kid in a high-tech playground.

"So what's the plan of attack?" I asked when Flick got off the phone. Her desk was the only one in the office that looked lived in. She'd even brought in an aspidistra and some framed pictures of her friends and family, and she'd turned an old server case into a rudimentary filing cabinet with old scarves draped around it for decoration. It sounded crazy and it was, but it actually looked pretty cool. She smiled and licked her lips.

"Well," she said. "That's the thing, isn't it? I don't know yet. All I know is that I've got four days to get as many journalists to come here as possible. Any ideas are more than welcome."

"Free beer should do it," I said.

"That's not a bad idea," Flick laughed. "I doubt that John would sign it off, though." The founder, who'd been listening to our conversation whilst working on a presentation for potential investors, looked up from his screen.

"That's fine by me," he said. "Just do what it takes. It's time for us to hit the big leagues, and it's time for you to earn your keep. We're ready to go international. We've got good growth in most of the Western world, but that's not enough. We're starting with Chinese. We're still below the radar of the government, so we'll open up now to make the most of it before they raise that damn firewall and ban us because we're not Chinese nationals."

"So much for free speech," said Flick.

"Speech is never free," John said. "It's expensive. They won't ignore us for long, but it'd be good to get a foothold if we can. They can't censor the internet forever, and we'll be right there when they lift the filter. Next, we look to India. Abhi is chipping in some overtime to work on the translations, and we're looking for another developer to help him to launch the new languages."

"Let me see the list of translations when you can, Boss," said Flick. "I've got an idea."

***

It turns out that Flick's idea was to launch another language – Pirate English, to be precise. Her reasoning was simple. People love pirates, ninjas and zombies, and zombie pirate ninjas most of all. Launching a language pack in Pirate English gave Former.ly a story, and journalists needed stories to survive. Our users were up for it, too. The results of our first research survey were in, and the consensus was that the site was too serious. We'd assumed that our users would be in a sombre mood when they accessed the site, but that couldn't have been further from the truth. Our users wanted the site to be a celebration of life – more like drinks at a wake than a stilted church service.

Besides, we'd done most of the hard work already. The functionality was well underway, and so we just needed to work through the translations – nothing major, just a list of terms from our interface and database and the piratisation of our help centre.

The list was long but not insurmountable, and I promised to give Flick a hand where I could. The first thing she did was to summon Abhi. John's timeline for the first new language was three weeks, but Flick wanted to cut that down to three days. She put the pressure on too. Within an hour, she'd pushed out a hurried press release, shouted from social media and called a couple of old friends who owed her enough favours to justify her ringing them on the weekend. By then, the wheels were in motion. Former.ly would be unveiling a new feature at their press event, a pirate party at the company's offices. I began to worry that getting people to attend was the least of our problems. Fitting them into the office could cause chaos, and she'd promised them a feature that we hadn't started building.

Still, we were a good team under pressure, and we holed up in the office for the rest of the weekend. Even Peter came in and worked late, mainly because Kerry was helping Flick to plan the event and so there was no one for him to hang out with. We pulled an all-nighter on Sunday and got a beta version up and running on our staging server, but it needed styling and the language packs were nowhere near completed. We managed to outsource some of the Chinese translation to a company called Ward Communications, but even at a premium and with all of their available resources, they were going to struggle to have it ready in time for our deadline. We needed it by noon on Tuesday to get it checked by a third party and then added to the site. There was no time for proper testing. We planned to get it up and running and then ask users for feedback along the way.

But I enjoyed it. I love a challenge. By Tuesday, we were turning up to work with sleeping bags and passing out under our desks or in the boardroom. That evening, Flick and I shared a couple of bottles of wine and tried to roll out the language pack for Pirate English. Flick was living a dual life. By day, she was working on the launch event, which was invite-only and a hard sell. By night, she worked on the translations and picked up any pieces that were left over.

That evening, when I was drunk, exhausted and emotional, I kissed her. Maybe she kissed me, I don't know. We went from sitting side by side to climbing on top of each other in a heartbeat. I looked at her, and she looked at me, and that was it. We didn't have sex, but we slept together, curled up in each other's arms in a shared sleeping bag. When we woke up again in the cold light of day, we put the evening behind us. There was work to do.

***

It was the day of the press event, and we were all exhausted and still stacked in an effort to get the new feature out of the door. It was working as well as could be expected, but there were still a bunch of bugs and we were already aware of dozens of amends that needed to be made. Still, it worked well enough for a demonstration, and we planned to launch it the following day if we ran into any last minute problems and had to delay it. It was ready, but it was also untested.

The first guests arrived at seven o'clock, despite the fact that we didn't kick off until eight. Flick had hired a bar for the evening, and she'd even managed to hook up sponsorship from a vodka company that liked our philosophy. Abhi and I were implementing the last of the last-minute fixes, but we accepted Flick's offer of drinks at our desks. We continued to work until the office was too busy to focus in and then shut down and stashed our gear away just as the lighting was lowered and Flick grabbed a microphone.

"Ladies and gentlemen, boys and girls," she announced. "Thank you very much for coming, and welcome to the party. My name's Felicity, but you can call me Flick. I'll be your host for the evening. Oh, and say hello to the internet!

Keep an eye out for Kerry. He's streaming us live across the globe, so make sure you're not caught doing anything you shouldn't be doing.

"I see that some of you read the memo about fancy dress," she continued, gesturing at a horde of drunken pirates who were watching her with their glasses raised. "And some of you did not," she added, aiming her remarks at a dozen dour-faced journalists who'd showed up in evening wear. I guessed, correctly, that they were from the broadsheets, and not from the tech press.

"Now," she said. "You're probably wondering why we asked you to dress up as pirates. I'm going to talk to you about that in a minute, but first, I'd like to introduce the company's co-founder, John Mayers." The crowd applauded, and Flick handed John the microphone. He looked terrible, like he hadn't slept in weeks. I suspected he probably hadn't.

"Thanks, Flick," he began, looking short and uncomfortable with the eyes of the crowd upon him. "And thanks to you guys for coming. Former.ly is not just a website. Former.ly is the fountain of youth, a way to find eternal life like no other. We've released immortality for free to the English-speaking world, and the world itself has responded. This weekend, we hit fifty million users, and we confirmed our eleven thousandth death. That's eleven thousand real people immortalised with their self-constructed memorials on our website. And, better still, we're growing at an alarming rate. I can't tell you who we're working with, but we're also taking on investment and expanding. Hence our brand new office. Do you like it?"

The crowd erupted in a cheer for a few seconds, which John took as an opportunity to take a swig from a bottle of water. He smiled as the noise faded away.

"Thank you," he said. "It's not finished yet, but we're on

our way. We're also taking on new staff – a new developer, an accountant and a couple of interns. They're here tonight, but behave yourselves. They're newbies, and we don't normally allow newbies to meet strangers. We've got a brand new feature to announce, but first I want to give you guys some metrics." By now, the office was awash with the light from dozens of handheld devices, from iPhones and iPads to Nexus tablets, Macbooks, and even a couple of Blackberries.

"So," John said, "fifty million users, and eight million monthlies. The site has been visited from three hundred million unique IP addresses in over a hundred different countries. We've helped to solve a murder case in Germany, to reunite a family in Israel, and to bring closure to thousands of grieving friends and relatives. We'll be releasing an infographic and a full chart-by-chart report of key analytics in our blog over the next couple of days, so keep your eyes peeled for that. In the meantime, please welcome Flick back to the stage to tell you about our brand new feature!"

The crowd applauded again and a couple of people slipped off to get another drink, but most of them stuck around to listen to Flick as she reclaimed the microphone.

"Ladies and gentlemen, you are pirates for a reason," she said. "At midnight tonight, our new user interface will become available in two new languages, one of which is Pirate English."

At first, there was silence. Then, someone laughed and the applause started up again. From towards the back, someone shouted, "Is this a joke?"

John grabbed the microphone from Flick and scowled at the heckler. "It's not a joke," he said. "Take us seriously or get out of here."

Flick looked up from her phone, which she'd been using

to tweet a photo of the audience, and took the microphone back. She looked sheepish.

"The bad news," Flick continued, "is that you're going to have to stick around to find out what the other language is. "The developers are still working on it." The audience laughed, but I dragged my hand across my throat from the back of the room, hoping it'd shut her up. Even Flick didn't know how close to the bone her remark was.

"The good news," she continued, "is that there's plenty of beer left. John will be back with an announcement at midnight. Until then, enjoy the DJ!"

***

At ten minutes to midnight, the party was still going strong, although half of the visitors had disappeared. John was being interviewed by TheNextWeb. I recognised one of Sarah's colleagues, a guy called Alex who I'd got drunk with a couple of times, but I hadn't seen her yet. Flick had been schmoozing all evening, and Kerry had been live-streaming the event on our home-page – a brave decision. Abhi had barely spoken except to thank a journalist who'd complimented his Rackspace T-shirt, so I was on my own. As a result, I spent most of the night drinking and talking to people I'd never met before. In the end, I pulled up in a corner to check my e-mails and to catch up with a couple more fixes.

I didn't look up until midnight when John returned to the microphone to make his announcement. By that time, the crowd had started to thin out and the rowdy collection of journalists, bloggers and tech geeks had spread out across the office, using any available space to prop up tablet computers and skinny laptops. Sarah showed up late and was too busy working to talk to me; I felt almost camouflaged, and no one paid me any attention.

"Ladies and gentlemen, thank you once again for coming," John bellowed. "Now, I'm sure you're all dying to know why we brought you here. It's time to open up to the world. China first, followed by India, Mainland Europe and the rest of the world. Tonight, right now, we're launching in Chinese. Get ready, world. We're coming."

Some of the audience members gasped. Those who'd stayed sober knew what that meant, and it had the potential to be one of the month's top stories. John waited several seconds to allow his statement to sink in before he continued.

"See, demand from China is high, so we're complying with local law when necessary. We have no desire to let something as artificial as politics interfere with our passion to connect the world in life and death. You guys were here at the beginning, at the international birth of Former.ly."

He laughed, paused for a moment and then asked, "Any questions?"

***

I woke up fully clothed on my sofa. There was no sign of Sarah, and I'm pretty sure I didn't come home with her the night before. She showed up late, stayed for half an hour and then went for a couple more drinks with her colleagues. Either way, I didn't care. I couldn't remember everything, but I still held a strange feeling of self-righteousness, as though I'd done nothing to be ashamed of. Perhaps I hadn't.

The night had left its mark on me, and I was desperate for some orange juice and a cooked breakfast. Former.ly wasn't through the storm yet, though. New users already flooding in, and the language packs were patchy at best and more like a beta than a full release. Peter was worried about the infrastructure, but John insisted that half a new feature was better than no new feature at all. All in all, we were flying on the seat of our pants and venturing rapidly into unexplored territory. Even John and Peter had never worked on anything like this before.

I was running ten minutes late, but that was hardly unusual. No one was ever on time, not even the interns. What was unusual, though, was my reception. Flick texted me to tell me to hurry up, and John's bright red face greeted me as soon as I stepped over the threshold and into the office.

"Where the hell have you been?" he demanded, pushing the door to slam it shut behind me.

"Sorry I'm late, Boss," I said. "The Underground was busy and the streets were packed. I got here as quickly as I could. What's wrong? Are there bugs in the release?"

"Forget the update," he replied. "There's been a murder. Alex, the guy from TheNextWeb. Some sort of poison, apparently. The police have already been to see me."

CHAPTER SEVEN

THE WEEK PASSED by in a blur of activity. Flick was working overtime to deal with the extra publicity, and Abhi and I were trying to stabilise the site. We were so busy that John called in the interns and agreed to start paying them a full-time wage. We still didn't know where that money was coming from.

The police showed up again on Saturday afternoon. They'd called by the flat to find that no one was home, so they followed John's trail to the office. There, they spoke to him in private, but he called a team meeting as soon as they left because he knew we wouldn't be able to do any work until we knew what was happening.

"You've probably noticed that the police are sniffing around," he told us. "I hate the police, but let them sniff. We've got nothing to hide. I want you guys to cooperate with them and to answer any questions that they ask you, but don't let them touch our hardware without consulting Peter first. Are we clear?"

We all murmured our assent.

"Good. It has nothing to do with us, so we'll let them get on with their investigation and keep our noses clean. They can check out the premises, they can speak to the staff and to the people who showed up, but they can't touch the servers or go through our code. I won't stand for it."

"Why would they need to do that?" I asked.

"They wouldn't," John replied. "But you can never be

too careful."

Satisfied that we understood him, John grunted and waved us back to our stations. We all got straight back to work. I had a hell of a lot of coding to do, and the murder had caused a PR disaster that Flick now had to deal with.

They say there's no such thing as bad publicity. I didn't know about that, but we were sure as hell hitting the headlines. To add further irony, the journalist's profile went live on our website, revealing his unhealthy obsession with one of his co-workers. The woman was never named, but I secretly suspected it was Sarah. She might be a bitch, but she's also beautiful. She could turn my head even when I was sick of the sight of her.

But the whole furore was made even worse on Sunday afternoon. An influential blogger started to speculate about the site and its operations, accusing John and Peter of defrauding the investors and describing them as "morally bankrupt". The article went viral, and the boys refused to issue a response, which only fuelled the mystery that seemed to surround us.

"I hate this guy," murmured Flick, putting the phone down at the end of a particularly stressful conversation. "Why can't he just keep his mouth shut? That's the problem with the internet. Anyone can post this shit without a single shred of evidence."

I glanced over. "Is he telling the truth?" I asked. She stared at me for a second, stuffed a wad of gum into her mouth and started chewing.

"Who cares?" she replied. "That's not the point. All I care about is putting out the fires that he started. Thank God that the mainstream press hasn't picked up on it. Even Mashable and TechCrunch are suspiciously quiet. Either they haven't heard about it yet or…"

"Or what?" I prompted. Flick thought for a while and

then shrugged.

"I don't know. Maybe Peter paid them off. More likely, they just don't care. Palo Alto's where it's at. If you're a start-up, you don't exist until you've got an office there."

"Then what the hell are we doing in London?" I asked.

***

The wave of publicity hit home on Monday morning, when the world's reporters returned to the office after a weekend of reality. TheNextWeb was the first publication to cover the rumours around the death of its former employee. Things quietened down for a couple of hours, and then the first vlogs appeared on YouTube; TechCrunch put out an article an hour or so later. By five PM, we'd been covered by Mashable, BBC News and the New York Times.

I felt bad for Sarah. TheNextWeb had her writing eulogies for her former colleague, and they hadn't even buried him yet. The police had held his body back for an autopsy, which left her and the rest of her team on edge. She cried a lot, and she stayed late at the office, but in a roundabout way, the death of her boss had led to a de facto promotion. She must've been in mixed minds – on the one hand, this was the biggest scoop of her life, and on the other, she'd lost a colleague. And now she had his old job and had to follow on from him. That's never easy at the best of times.

We hit the half-life of the storm just after midnight, but the pandemonium continued until the following Wednesday, and the fallout lasted until after Christmas. John was absolutely furious. I'd never seen him in such a rage. Luckily, he channelled it into his work. He even started sleeping in the office. By contrast, even though the workload was heavy, Abhi and I were usually at home by nine.

It was at around this time that Elaine joined the team.

She was a bad fit from the start, fifty-three years old with three kids and a grandchild on the way. She joined us to bring our accounts in order. John said it was a temporary arrangement, but she ended up staying on.

Even though she was only in for a couple of days a week, we quickly got used to seeing her around. She reminded us that we were human and that failure is inevitable and will come to all of us, eventually. In return, we helped her out with tech support. She struggled with Mac OS on a daily basis. Wonderful woman, though.

One day, when the work was slow and the atmosphere subdued, I was sitting in the office with Flick, Abhi, Kerry, Elaine and the two interns when John and Peter burst into the room and told us to gather round.

"Guess what?" Peter grinned. He was back in the office after another stint in the States, and his leathery face bore the signs of long days in the sun. Apparently, Peter's deals were struck and sealed with high fives in the swimming pool. John didn't bother to wait for us to answer. He just dived right in with the good news.

"The money came through," he announced, staring us down from his spot at the head of the assembly. "The investment is official. We're on the books. Your jobs are safe for another year, if you behave yourselves."

"That's right," Peter said. "Get it out there, Flick. No embargo. We're in business. Let's show the world that we've got something to say."

"So what happens next?" I asked when the hubbub died down. "What does the future hold for Former.ly?"

John grinned. "I guess you'll have to wait and see," he said.

***

By the end of the following week, we were riding high on a wave of self-confidence that was buoyed by overwhelming feedback from both the press and the general public. We received particular support from the families of our users. We'd helped thousands of grieving mothers to gain closure, and the children and spouses of the dead often discovered messages of love from beyond the grave.

One case in particular caught the public's imagination – a troubled young musician, who died injecting methamphetamine into a vein on the back of his knee. The media vilified him, portraying him as a drug-crazed narcissist who cared about nothing except for drugs, booze and money, but then his profile went live and revealed a different side to him. He'd updated it religiously, as often as a dozen times a day, and it was full of beautiful lyrics and haunting melodies. Flick followed the whole story with a kind of morbid fascination as it played out on our servers and in the pages of the gossip magazines.

"Basically," she explained, "he was in love with his best friend's wife. He desperately wanted to tell her, but he couldn't."

"Why not?" I asked, feigning interest.

"Because the best friend was also in the band," she said. "Poor guy. He had an obsession. She was all he ever wrote about. He even blamed her for his addiction. Turns out that she felt the same way. She went into mourning and left her husband, and now all three of them are fucked up. It's sad, really, how a drug can ruin three lives in one evening."

"He brought it on himself," I told her. I was in a bad mood. The site's messy variables were beginning to get under my skin. I kept having weird dreams where they danced back and forth on the screen, changing from Chinese to French to Arabic every time I blinked or looked away. By now, Flick could tell when I wasn't happy, so she looked at me sternly and pursed her lips together.

"Perhaps," she said, eventually. "All I know is that, as cynical as it sounds, his death has been a blessing for the company. We're bringing in new users from all over the world. In America and Australia in particular. It's insane. We've never seen growth like this before, not since the company started. The only way is up!"

"Yeah," I scoffed. "As long as the servers and the code hold it together. Right now, I'm not so sure they can."

CHAPTER EIGHT

CHRISTMAS WAS A QUIET AFFAIR. For the first time in years, Sarah and I didn't see each other. She went to stay with her family, but I had no time for mine. I spent most of the holidays working on the front end and drinking cheap lager in front of the TV. I know that doesn't sound like much, but it was good enough for me. I didn't even realise it was New Year's Eve until the fireworks started to go off. An exhausted end to a busy year.

We were officially back in the office on the second of January. John and Peter were reluctant to give us the bank holiday, but they hadn't had much of a choice. I went in there anyway to get out of the flat, but I was the only one there other than the two founders, and I left early because their occasional arguments drove me crazy whenever Flick wasn't around. She seemed to have a calming, neutralising effect on the group. We needed it the following day. John ordered yet another team meeting and then erupted as soon as we were all together.

"Guys, just a heads up," he scowled. "The flat was broken into last night while we were sleeping. Luckily, the sight of Kerry on the sofa was enough to scare them off. We were just lucky he was still awake. That man will sleep through anything."

"Thanks, Boss," Kerry grinned. John didn't look amused.

"Indeed. It looks like sometimes you do have your uses.

Listen, guys, we need to double down on security. Don't bring anyone to the office unless you trust them. Flick, that goes for journalists too."

"Oh man," she murmured. "You've got to be kidding me. This place is one of our greatest assets. Where do you expect me to take them?"

"Take them out for a coffee or a bite to eat," John replied. "Our budget can stretch to that, just about. Keep it locked down tight at home too. We don't know who they were or what they were looking for, but we can take a good guess. A lot of people would like to see us fail."

"John," Elaine said, holding out a hand for silence. The two founders respected Elaine for her financial brains, if not for her entrepreneurial spirit, and they always had time for her. "Don't you think you're being paranoid? You should report it to the police."

"I don't want the police sniffing around here," he replied. "We keep things private. That's just how we roll. As for being paranoid, I don't know. I'm just very aware that our servers contain a hell of a lot of sensitive data. People would kill to get at it. No more working from home, either. Everything stays on Peter's servers."

The development team groaned in unison. We all knew what that meant. Here was a job that you could never complete inside of hours, and now we couldn't even work from home. This was going to mean a lot of long evenings at the office.

"I know," John said, spreading his hands defensively. "It's not ideal. But our hands are tied. Shit's getting real, folks. Just make sure you keep it tight and everything will be fine. We're getting some help in too. Peter's got a friend who specialises in security, and we trust him. We're going to see about bringing him in. Until then, all other hires are on hold. That's all for now. Let's get back to work."

***

Peter flew back the following day. John got hold of him on the phone when he was making his way through passport control, and he wasted no time in telling him about the break-in. In a panic, Peter jumped straight into a cab at the airport and travelled directly to the office, where we'd ordered pizza to celebrate his return. He wolfed down a couple of slices, wiped the grease from his hands and walked straight into the cramped boardroom for a private meeting with John.

The two founders never told us what they talked about, but I had a pretty good guess. Over the next couple of days, Peter worked around the clock to move the servers to a new, more secure location – one that was reliable and unlikely to cause any downtime. Even John wasn't to know where they were. Peter claimed to have found a way to store them with complete anonymity, referring to it as a temporary fix until our new head of security could join us.

But even with the servers stored securely in some mysterious lock-up in the middle of nowhere, the founders weren't happy. Then, one gloomy Thursday afternoon, Abhi took me aside to tell me he was thinking about leaving the company.

"I just can't keep up," he said. "My wife is upset because I don't spend any time with her. And now we have a child on the way."

"Wow, congratulations," I said, wrapping my arms around his shoulders. Inwardly, I felt the pity that comes naturally to the childless when they secretly wonder why all of their friends are having children when it's such an inconvenience.

"Thanks," he replied. "You're the first person I've told.

John would tell me I'm crazy."

"That depends on what you've got lined up after Former.ly. And on when you're planning on leaving. We'll be in a lot of trouble without you."

"I know. You're stuck with me for a while, yet. I told Sonal to give me until after the birth to take paternity leave so I can look for a new job."

"And you think your leave will be granted?" I asked.

"Hell no. But whatever. You understand that this conversation never happened, yes?"

"Of course," I replied. "Your secret's safe with me." I seemed to be saying that a lot of late.

***

Peter became unbearable after the break-in. He insisted that someone needed to be at both the office and the flat at all times, which was both insane and impractical. It meant that Kerry had to stay at the flat and work from there, while John had to sleep at the office. When John was away, Flick and I took in sleeping bags and kept each other company through the long, dark nights. But not in that way. Aside from our drunken kiss at the end of the previous year, Flick and I stayed as friends and split the duty of guarding the office so that neither of us was ever left alone amidst the hum of the computers.

One night, as we lay there in the boardroom, I heard a noise from outside the office. I couldn't sleep, and Flick lay wide-awake beside me on the hardwood floor.

"What was that?" she whispered. I cursed softly and wrapped my hands around the baseball bat that John had ordered me to sleep beside.

"You heard it too? Damn it, that means I'll have to check it out." My voice was husky and half-muffled with exhaustion, but Flick was shrill and full of adrenaline. She grabbed my wrist and stared urgently into my eyes.

"Be careful out there," she said. "Don't get yourself hurt."

"Thanks," I replied, "for staying positive."

"I'm serious, Dan. Former.ly needs you. I need you, you idiot."

"Don't worry. I'll be back," I told her. "I promise." She smiled reassuringly as I wriggled out of my sleeping bag and shuffled towards the door. The noises seemed louder now. I could make out a couple of different voices from the alleyway outside, and they didn't sound friendly. I scouted out the office and saw nothing, so I sidled over to the window, opened it slowly and poked my head out into the cool night air.

From here, I could see them clearly, silhouetted by the streetlights. There were three of them, riding on bicycles with scarves around their necks to disguise their faces and to keep them warm in the bitter weather. I watched them for a couple of seconds – for long enough to figure out that they were digging through our bins in search of something – and then remembered that I was supposed to be defending the place. I flipped, partly because Flick was watching me from the boardroom, and I shouted at them from the safety of a second floor window.

"Hey! What the hell do you think you're doing?" The youths looked up at me and they laughed en masse. Then, one of them broke off from the group and launched a projectile at the window. The glass shattered on impact, and I fell backwards under the assault, brushing broken glass off my tracksuit bottoms. I cursed under my breath and then stepped gingerly through the glass in my bare feet so that I could lean through the window again.

The youths had bottled it, and they were already on

their bikes and halfway down the alleyway. "Get back here right now," I bellowed, secretly hoping they'd ignore me. "You little shits."

But it was too late. They were out of sight in a matter of seconds. I was glad. It didn't take much to shout at people from the safety of a building, but I didn't want a confrontation. I was just glad that they were gone, and that I'd saved face in front of Flick.

I made my way back to the boardroom and climbed into my sleeping bag. Flick was already in there, waiting for me.

***

We didn't get much sleep that night, what with one thing and another, so we were both glad when Abhi arrived the following morning. A light rain had filtered in through the broken window and left discoloured patches on the carpet. Shards of broken glass were scattered across a six-foot square, and the offending object had bounced across the room and stumbled to a halt in front of the beanbags. I'd examined it earlier that morning – some sort of tinned food with the label removed. I thought I'd better leave the scene as it was in case John wanted to see it. Knowing him, he probably would.

It was cold as hell in the winter when the fires go out, and even with multiple layers of clothing, we were still freezing. We turned the heating up as high as it would go, but the cold wind blew in from outside and circulated through the office. But there wasn't much that we could do. John would want to see the scene before he decided what to do with it.

When Abhi arrived, he took one look around the office and collapsed into his chair. "What happened?" he asked.

"Good question," I growled. "We were attacked in the

middle of the night. I tried to scare some kids who were going through the bins. It didn't turn out so good."

"I can see that," he replied. "What will the boss say?"

"Who cares what John says?" Flick scowled. Her eyes were dark with lack of sleep, but she seemed stronger now and in charge of the situation. "If he'd been here, then Dan wouldn't have had to deal with it. He's just going to have to tap those investors for some cash for a new window."

"And have you called the police?"

"Of course not," I replied. "You heard what the boss said. He doesn't want them poking around. No, if he wants to call the cops, he can do it himself."

John came back later that afternoon. He took the news surprisingly well. "At least they didn't get in here," he said, booting up his laptop and settling down at his workstation. "And we don't throw out our paperwork; we burn it. You guys have been running a tight ship, so thanks for that."

"But who were they?" asked Abhi. "And what did they want? Are you sure that we're safe here?"

"Abhi, we're just off one of the busiest streets in the city, and we've kitted the place out like a fortress. You're safer here than you are at home."

I disagreed. "You say that, but no one's throwing tinned food at my bedroom window, Boss. Abhi's got a point."

John thought for a moment before making his decision. "Okay," he said. "You win. We'll call in some reinforcements. We'll sign the deal with Peter's friend's security firm. Your safety is paramount to the success of the site. I'm not going to lie. We need you."

CHAPTER NINE

JOHN WASN'T KIDDING when he said he was stepping up security. Peter flew back from Palo Alto a couple of days later, and his "security advisor," a stocky bodybuilder called Nils, joined us shortly afterwards. He didn't talk much. He was an ex-army type with slight paranoia and a keen eye for detail. A nice guy, once you got to know him.

Nils, John and Peter locked themselves away for a couple of days to form a war committee and then re-emerged with stern faces and a series of baffling charts, diagrams and spreadsheets which they claimed would be enough to guarantee our security.

"It's going to be great," babbled John, as he showed Nils around the office for the first time. "Guys, this is Nils. He's going to scare away the bad guys."

"Who exactly are the bad guys?" Nils asked. John laughed.

"That's just it, Nils. We don't know. They don't exactly carry business cards. Part of your job will be to find out who they are and to stop them by any means necessary."

"That's only part of it?"

"Yeah," John said. "We work hard here. You'll also take over the CCTV system and the alarms. Don't worry about the servers. Peter looks after those. He's the only person who even knows where they are. You'll also be in charge of out-of-hours security. Form a team that you trust and then set up a watch. I want protection around the clock for both the office and the flat. Guarding them ourselves just isn't going to cut it. We need professionals. Think you can manage it?"

Nils grinned, a huge expansive smile that oozed self-confidence and quiet mastery. It made me feel uncomfortable.

"Well that depends," he replied. "What's your budget?"

"Tell us what you need and we'll see what we can do. This is top priority. Secure the place and find out who's trying to mess with us. We'll cover any reasonable costs. Until we know who they are, our hands are tied. How do you fight a shadow?"

Silence descended upon the room. Even Elaine was staring at John with rapt attention. His words had hit home. We just didn't know what we were going to do. As always, Former.ly's future was uncertain.

***

Nils stayed true to his word, and within two weeks he'd assembled a squad to guard the two premises around the clock. There was talk of getting dogs at both locations too. Flick, of course, was thrilled by the prospect of having an animal in the office.

"Think of the PR value in that," she said. "Marketing is about telling stories, and this could be a great one."

"I'm not talking about a cocker spaniel, Flick." Nils had a way of speaking which made everyone else feel like an idiot. "I'm talking about an Alsatian or a bulldog – maybe a retired police dog if we can get one. I'm talking about scaring the bastards. Put that one in your storybook."

Still, we felt safer with Nils around, even though he seemed to serve no practical purpose. Either way, I was too busy with my own problems. Abhi and I had been putting in long hours to follow John's vague orders to work on a new feature that the bosses wanted to keep under wraps until its launch. We hadn't been briefed about it, and our instructions still came in the form of a list of coded variables, but I'd been working at the company for long enough to be able to make a good guess at what I was working on.

My suspicions were confirmed the following week when John and Peter called the team together for another meeting. By now, our growth was beginning to show. We had one hell of a team. Two of our interns were now officially recognised as junior developers; the third one left, but John had recruited five more from his old university. Nils was there as well, and so were some of his men. There were always at least two of them in the office at any time of the day or night. Nils said it was so that there was always someone there to watch the watcher. Then there was Elaine, who was working flat out and needed frequent help from Flick and the founders just to stay on top of things, and the rest of the team. All in all, I counted fourteen people. Three months ago, there were six of us.

"Big news, boys and girls." When revealing things to the team, John always acted like a footballer or a rock 'n' roll star at a press conference. "We're monetising, baby!"

"That's right," grinned Peter. "It's time to start showing our investors that we can make some money."

"With adverts, right?" I asked. John glared at me. I took the hint and piped down.

"Yes," he sighed. "With adverts. Now, I know what you're thinking. Flick, this will affect you in particular. What are people going to think when they find out that a memorial site is running adverts?"

"They're going to be pretty pissed off, I imagine," Flick replied.

Peter smiled. "You hit the nail on the head, Flick. Our users are our lifeblood. We have to keep them on our side."

"So what are we going to do?" she asked.

"It's simple," replied John, taking control of the situation. "The adverts appear on the back end on the users' admin panels. That way, advertisers can market to the living. No ads will be displayed on the memorials of the deceased. We mean no disrespect."

"And what about the advertisers?" I asked. "Where do they come in?"

"We're launching a do-it-yourself system," Peter replied. "Which is what you and Abhi have been working on. When that launches, we can target small business. In the meantime, we've signed an exclusive deal with an insurance provider to get the first set of ads up and running. We're talking big money, and there's plenty more of it just waiting for us to reach out and take it."

Flick was on the edge of her seat. This was huge news, and it could change the company forever. When the adverts went live, we could become profitable within a couple of years, assuming our users didn't abandon us. Unfortunately, in situations like these, you have to push the updates live and hope for the best.

***

Two days later, I overheard an intense conversation between the two founders while I was tucked away in the toilet. They entered the room in the middle of a heated discussion. It sounded like they'd been talking for a while.

"Damn it, John," Peter was saying. "I don't like it. What happens if the users revolt? If we lose the users, we lose the site."

"We don't have a choice," John snapped. "We're cleaned out, Pete. If we don't start making money soon, we're finished anyway. We've got to do something."

"Can't we take on more investment? Cut overheads?"

"Who's going to invest in us if we don't prove we can make some money?"

"True," Peter agreed. "But ads? I hate ads. I never thought we'd sell out." I couldn't see them, but I could picture John's reaction as clearly as if he'd been standing in front of me. His cheeks always flushed when he was angry, and Peter pissed him off. When John replied, his voice was calm and monotone. He was clearly making an effort.

"Me neither," he replied. "I didn't think we'd get this far. But now we're here, if we don't continue then everything was pointless."

"Death is always pointless, John. Don't act like you give a damn about the dead. You just don't want to fail."

"And you don't want to fail either," John snapped. "Let's face it. You're in just as deep as I am. You'd better hope that no one finds out what we're up to. Be careful with who you trust. There could be a mole inside the company for all we know. And look after yourself in Palo Alto."

I waited for the two founders to leave and then gave it an extra five minutes, just in case. I didn't want anyone to know what I'd heard. It was hard enough to keep my head down.

***

That evening, Sarah and I shared a rare moment of solitude. These days, we were more like friends than lovers, partly because we never saw each other, but we still shared the bed when we were both at home, and we did a little more than that after a bottle of wine and a pleasant conversation.

We were cuddled up on the sofa with two bottles of rosé and six cans of Stella, content to chill in front of the TV with a takeaway pizza. As always, the conversation turned to work, and I was just telling Sarah about the conversation I'd overheard when I realised that her eyes had glazed over and she wasn't listening.

"What's the matter?" I asked. She took a swig from her wine and then looked away to refill her glass.

"I'm just sick of it, Dan. Former.ly, Former.ly, Former.ly. That's all you ever talk about. I remember when you used to talk about me – about my work and my life."

"It's not my fault if you never want to talk about it," I replied. "You're always too tired."

"That's not the point," she snapped. "And you know it. We never spend any time together because we're both so busy. I love having my own life and I know you've got your own stuff to deal with, but a girl needs to feel special from time to time."

"I'll try harder," I promised. She held my hand and pressed closer.

"But don't you see, Dan? You shouldn't have to try. You should do it automatically. And that's the problem."

"What do you mean?" I asked. The alcohol was starting to get to me, and I needed to go to the toilet. Sarah sighed.

"Tomorrow's my birthday," she said. "And we haven't even mentioned it. Had you forgotten?"

"Of course not," I lied. "I'm taking you out for dinner after work if you can make it?"

"I thought you'd never ask," she said. "I'll be there."

***

Of course, life doesn't work like that. It's like there's a constant curse that follows me around. An Israeli research firm reported a major security flaw, and John made us stay until the fix went live. In all fairness, we were lucky that the bug was found by good guys. We were offering cash rewards for amateurs who submitted bug reports, but the money that we paid out was a pittance in comparison to the damage that a hacker could do.

We got the bug fixed after working in a team of four to replicate and annihilate the problem, but it was still just after nine by the time that we were finished. I left straight afterwards, but Abhi stayed late to work on his main project, a refinement to the advertising dashboard. It still hadn't gone live, and there was going to be hell to pay if it wasn't ready by the weekend. But that wasn't my problem. I had my own deadlines to worry about.

I called Sarah to let her know I was running late, and she gave me an earful down the telephone line. I decided to stop off on my way back home to pick up some flowers, not realising that she wouldn't be there to receive them.

To make matters worse, I got stuck in commuter traffic and didn't get back to the flat until ten. I was supposed to be meeting Sarah two hours earlier, but after the second call to let her know I was going to be even later, she refused to pick up the phone. I was hardly surprised that she wasn't there. She had, however, left a note. It didn't look good.

"Dan," it began. Her handwriting was hurried, and she'd written the message on a series of Post-it Notes that she'd attached, one after the other, to the TV screen. "You've got some explaining to do. When I said no excuses, I meant it. I waited as long as I could, but I gave up and went out with the girls instead. Let's talk about this tomorrow. I'm not impressed."

CHAPTER TEN

FOR A WHILE, my life seemed to settle down. Work was busy but bearable, money was scarce but sufficient, and Sarah and I had made up, broken up and made up again. I'd even gone for dinner with her and her parents, even though I hate them. They're too conservative, and they think that she's wasting her time with TheNextWeb. They say that she's not a real journalist until her work appears in print. The fools can't see that the printed word is as old and as frail as they are.

As for me, I was proud of her, in a way. But mainly, I didn't give a damn about her job, as long as it kept her busy. If she was busy, she wouldn't have the time to nag me about the hours I put in at Former.ly.

As the weather grew warmer and we slowly left the winter behind, Former.ly released its advertisements to general indifference. Big brands stuck with Google, Facebook and other more mainstream options.

"Part of that is down to the nature of the site," Flick explained. "People don't want to associate their brand with death."

Local businesses, meanwhile, loved it. We got a lot of business from funeral homes and florists, as well as from restaurants, mom-and-pop stores and even from some of the more entrepreneurial franchises that ignored corporate guidelines and decided to try something new.

Our users barely noticed the addition of the adverts,

although the media claimed that they were leaving in droves. The truth is, they had no idea about what was going on at the company, and Former.ly lied to everyone. On our end, we knew that we were growing faster than ever before, and existing users were logging in more often and for longer. In fact, we were doing just fine, but it couldn't hurt if people thought we were struggling. It gave us the element of surprise whenever we decided to prove them wrong.

But we still weren't profitable – at least, not yet. We were taking in money, but it wasn't enough to cover the servers and our overheads. The investors were still funding our salaries and barely 5 percent of our ad slots were being filled. The click through rate was pretty good and most of our customers were happy with the results, but it wasn't exactly perfect.

We didn't have much time to work on updates, though. We were already rolling out new features at a blistering speed. We'd released an iPhone app after working with developers from a specialist agency, but that wasn't enough. Peter had taken on the challenge of recruitment, and we planned to build an in-house team to work on smartphone and tablet applications for iOS and Android. We hadn't made a hire yet, but we were close.

"Mobile isn't the future," Peter told us. "But it is the past and the present, and it's here to stay. We're going to work on an SMS-based service too. Then, we launch in India. Abhi's already translated all of the language packs."

The developer nodded his acknowledgement, but I caught a stirring of resentment in his movements. He'd been acting strangely of late, and I think I know why. He was worried about the future. So was I, come to think of it.

***

As March gave way to April, the servers went down again. Luckily, we'd upgraded our infrastructure and so only the U.S. was affected. I say "only." John was absolutely furious.

"What the hell, Pete?" he demanded, glaring at him over the top of a computer screen. John had only just found out about the outage because he'd been out of the office in a meeting. Peter, for his part, had stopped by on his way to the airport. "Why are our servers down again? Do you want us to lose our users?"

"I'm on it, John. Calm down, these things happen. We're growing too quickly to be invincible. And there's good news too. It's not a Denial of Service attack, if that's what you think. We were already close to capacity, and then some articles went up that pushed us over the edge."

"Don't worry, Boss," said Flick. "I'll get right on it. We need to keep the lines of communication open so that people know what's going on. I reckon we can control the fallout, but only if we act now."

"So what are you waiting for? Get on it. You should be doing this already. The rest of you, get back to work. You don't get paid to sit around all day. Except for you, Elaine. You come with me."

***

That night, we foiled another break-in. Nils suspected one of his men of taking a bribe and launched a review of personnel. Nothing was taken and no damage was done, but the whole place was turned over in the middle of the night. One of the guards was knocked unconscious, and another was found bound and gagged in the alley outside.

Peter was furious because we had no way of knowing whether our data had been compromised. We didn't think so, but how could we be sure? Nils's CCTV cameras caught four figures dressed from head to toe in black, like the guy from *The Princess Bride*. They rushed in, overpowered the two guards and sprayed paint over the cameras. That's the last we saw of them, which gave them around two hours in the office before the cleaners disturbed them.

"My men saw nothing," said Nils, addressing us in our temporary war room. "But I don't know if I can trust them. Either way, don't worry. I'm looking into it."

"Worry?" laughed Flick. "Two of your men could have been killed! And you think it might have been an inside job? For all we know, the people we're trusting to protect us are being paid by someone else to try to kill us!"

"Yeah," I agreed. "And why are we even paying you in the first place? What's the point in having security guards if they're going to get themselves knocked out at the first sign of trouble?"

"And where were you, Dan?" Nils snapped. "They're brave lads, whether you trust them or not. I'll do some digging because you can never be too careful, but my priority is to find out how they got into the building in the first place. I'll step up security, too."

"I wonder," John murmured. The conversation had descended into chaos, and I was the only one who seemed to hear him. "Perhaps there's another solution."

***

The atmosphere in the office continued to darken over the next couple of days, and even a long weekend away on the coast wasn't enough to lift my spirits. That was part of Sarah's attempt to resurrect our relationship, to breathe a little life into something that neither of us really believed in. Oh sure, we got drunk together, and we wandered hand-in-hand along the seafront, but we were hiding a secret sadness from the world.

By the time I returned to the office, tensions were at breaking point. Peter was back from the States and in a foul mood, and John was acting like a man possessed. He had something up his sleeve, and we all knew it. He was bouncing around like Kerry after seven cups of coffee at a hackathon.

While Peter locked himself away in the boardroom, John ordered pizza and cracked open a case of beer, which got demolished in less than an hour.

"What's going on?" asked Abhi, lending his voice to the question on everybody's minds. John wrapped an arm around his shoulders and steered him randomly around as he paced the office.

"What's going on, Abhi? I'll tell you, shall I?" He paused for a second to crack open another beer before continuing. "We've got some big news. Bigger than anything that's ever happened to us before."

"Yes, sir," Abhi replied. "But you haven't actually said-"

"Don't break my stride," John scowled, holding his hand up for silence. "Where was I? Ah, yes, we're having a team meeting in five minutes, and I want all of you in it. Finish up whatever you're doing and follow me into the boardroom. Leave your phones, your tablets and your laptops behind. You won't need them. You won't even need a pen and paper. This is important. I want no distractions."

CHAPTER ELEVEN

THE BOARDROOM was pretty crowded, like a busy photograph or a bad painting. It was small at the best of times, walled off from the rest of the office behind a glass partition. The glass was still damaged from the pirate party, when a journalist had tried to walk through it. We laughed at the time, but somehow it earned us a bad write-up and a glassware bill of nearly £800. We'd decided not to pay it unless we had to.

I was pressed up against Flick and Abhi, right in the corner of the room. We'd been through enough team meetings by now to know that the safest place to be was as far away from John as possible. He wasn't exactly scary, just unpredictable, and it was an open secret that sitting at the front might get you fired. Flick learned that the hard way a couple of weeks back, and she hadn't come into the office for days. She only came back because Kerry convinced John to apologise.

The whole company turned out for the meeting. The original team had changed completely. By now, Abhi and I were reluctantly heading up our own division of developers, although John was still the boss. The founders had no idea that Abhi wanted to leave, and whilst I was happy to stick around, I wasn't ready for the responsibility – unfortunately, neither of us had any choice.

The two of us were walled into the boardroom by Nils and his men. They were part of the place by now, and we didn't even notice they were there unless they got in the way, which happened all the fucking time. I still didn't think they served a purpose, but John disagreed. As far as I was concerned, their investigation had failed and we were just as vulnerable as ever.

Elaine rounded off our motley crew, sitting front and centre on one of the half-dozen chairs that skirted the boardroom table. The air hummed with idle chatter and the faint stink of body odour. Cleanliness is never a priority when you're trying to change the world. Then, John raised his hand for silence, Peter closed the lid of his MacBook, and the hubbub began to die down.

"Are we ready, boys and girls? Good! Then let's begin."

***

"When Peter and I created Former.ly, we had a vision," John began. "We wanted to create a digital afterlife, a social network for the dead and for the living that they left behind."

"And that's exactly what we did, buddy!" Peter grinned. For once, John didn't seem annoyed at the interruption. In fact, he gave his co-founder a brief high five before continuing.

"You're right," John said. "That is what we did, and we did it well. From zero to half a million users in the first six months. Along the way, we hired our first developer. Abhi has been with us since the early days, and his hard work on the back end got us where we are today. Good work, Abhi!"

"You're welcome, Boss," Abhi said, as the rest of us launched into a round of applause. John smiled and waited for the applause to die down before continuing.

"With Abhi on board, we started rolling out serious new features and cleaning up the code. We left our closed beta, launched to the public and took on Kerry to shoot some tutorials and adverts. Kerry also cleaned up the UI and made the site look incredible. In fact, after we rolled out Kerry's first batch of updates, our conversion rate shot up and we started signing up new users at an alarming rate. By the end of our first year, we hit eight million users and registered hundreds of verified deaths. But it wasn't enough."

"It sure wasn't," Peter agreed. "Which was why we hired you, Flick." Flick grinned beside me and fired off a quick salute, which Peter returned half-heartedly.

"Flick joined us as our in-house marketing and PR whizz," John continued. "See, Peter and I are the visionaries. We can build a decent product, but we need someone like Flick to spread the word. Flick used to work for a PR agency, so we knew we had to have her. When you cross her brain with Kerry's camera, you're on to a winner. She bought into our vision and has worked tirelessly ever since to make us the fastest-growing social network this side of the pond. Good work, Flick!"

"Thanks, Boss," she replied. "But you forgot to mention that I'm the office manager too. Someone's got to keep things running."

"Of course," said John. "You're right. That's been a big part of what you've done for us. But you're more useful when you're pimping us out than when you're ordering the shopping and emptying the dishwasher. So guess what? We've got news for you. We're hiring another office manager, a proper one. She'll take all of the shit off your hands so you can concentrate on PR and marketing."

"Sounds good," said Flick. "When does she start?"

"Well, that depends," he replied. "We need to find her first. For now, just remember that we appreciate what you're doing. In fact, you made such a difference to the company that we had to hire Dan, our second developer."

I smiled but said nothing. I hate being the centre of attention, and I always have done. Luckily, John continued his monologue and all eyes returned to the front of the room.

"When Dan joined, things really started shaping up. He took over a lot of my duties, which allowed me to spend more time with Peter working on our strategy. We've got a lot to share with you, but that comes later. Until then, let's just say that if Dan hadn't joined us, most of you guys would be out of a job. Dan and Abhi here allowed us to start to develop our development team, and with a bit of luck it'll keep on growing as we add more features and branch out on to new platforms."

"But so far," said Peter, "we've only looked at the positives. There are downsides to running a business, like espionage. Ladies and gentlemen, let me tell you something that might surprise you. One of you is a spy."

***

After Peter's accusation, nobody moved for a full five seconds. It was clear from glancing around the room that this wasn't a revelation to his co-founder, but everyone else seemed shocked. Flick looked like she was ready to cry.

"That's right," said John, breaking the silence. "One of you has been leaking information to the press, and to God knows who else on top of that. We think we know who it is too. But first, has anyone got anything they'd like to say? An admission of guilt, perhaps?"

No such admission was forthcoming; most people just looked confused, but a couple of the newer members of the team were seething at the accusation. I wasn't surprised. Former.ly is a labour of love, but it doesn't treat you kindly. People usually either left within three months or stuck with it until the bitter end.

"Fair enough," John said. "But don't say I didn't warn you. Graham, step forward please." Obediently, one of the junior developers stood up and made his way to the front of the room. "Graham, do you deny that you've been opening that big mouth of yours? Someone's been leaking our movements – someone from inside the company. Someone with more brains than sense."

"No comment," he replied. You can say what you like about Graham (he was lazy, inept, and a bastard), but the guy had balls. John looked ready to punch him, and if looks could kill, then Nils would be well on the way to a jail cell.

"You can do this the easy way or the hard way," John said. "Leaking our movements was just the start of it, wasn't it? See, we figured something strange was going on when journalists showed up at places before we even arrived, and when people started writing about new features before we released them. It's funny, that – ever notice that none of those features got released?"

"Graham," Peter said, calmly. "We're not stupid. Why do you think we were never dumb enough to trust you with anything more than making widgets and crappy plug-ins? It's hard not to notice that the only features that ever got leaked were the ones that you came up with, or the fake ones that we've had you working on over the last six weeks. Where else would they have got that information? And here's the funny part – we're not even going to use them."

"No comment," he replied.

"Who have you been talking to?" John asked. There was no response. "You know how tight security is, Graham. You must have known that you'd get caught out. So why did you do it? Was it for the money?"

"No comment."

"We could have given you more. You could've changed

the world with us, Graham. Now you're barely even fit to be a user. Get out of here and don't come back, and don't even think about taking your machine. You're not going to need it where you're going."

"Whatever you say," Graham replied. "It's been fun." And that was that. Graham was ushered out of the room without any fuss, and John continued his speech about the importance of loyalty to the company. It was a moving speech, but I didn't pay much attention. Flick nudged me shortly after Graham's exit and nodded in the direction of the doorway.

One of our security guards, the big one with cauliflower ears and a scar on his upper lip, was skulking into the room with a lopsided grin on his face. I had a bad feeling about the guy, and besides, he kept massaging his knuckles. I knew first-hand how the founders hated to lose, and John seemed like the kind of guy who'd tell the world about his website whilst his heavies put the pressure on anyone who opposed him.

"So let that be a warning," John concluded, jerking me back to reality. "We will not tolerate indiscretion. Security is of paramount importance, and we can't afford to leak anything, whether you're talking to the press or whether you're chatting about your day to the wife and kids. Dan, you need to be more careful than most. Your girlfriend is a journalist, right?"

"She is," I replied. "She's one of the enemy. But we don't talk about work. In fact, we don't really talk about anything."

"Good," John replied. "That's how it should be. The same goes for the rest of you. Keep your mouths shut or I'll be showing you the door. Are we clear?"

As one, the employees murmured a grumpy acquiescence. It was enough for the two founders, who smiled.

"Good," said John. "That's what I was hoping for. Nils, sweep the room and lock it down. I want no electronics in here. It's time for a private announcement."

***

It took Nils and his men a good twenty minutes to scour the room for bugs, but we weren't complaining. We finished off the last of the pizza, cracked open a couple more beers and chatted amongst ourselves whilst we waited for the room to be secured. Turns out that we're basically an honest bunch. Once we knew the rules, we were all more than happy to hand over our equipment, and the search of the room turned up nothing but a faulty router. Truth was, we all wanted to hear what John had to say.

At last, John was satisfied. "Sorry about that," he said. "But we can't be too careful, and you'll be glad you stuck around."

"Get on with it," Flick murmured, so quietly that only I could hear it. I could feel the thrill of her breath on the back of my neck.

"You've probably noticed that Elaine has been spending more and more time in the office," John continued. "As of next Monday, she'll be joining the team full-time. We simply can't get by without her. There's too much money flowing in and out of the business, and we need to keep track of it. According to Elaine here, at one point we were three weeks away from defaulting on our payments, and that just won't do. Elaine will be joining us five days a week and bringing everything into shape, which brings me on to our next news. Peter, it's your contact. Want to take this one?"

"Sure thing," he replied, climbing carefully out of his chair. "Now, as many of you know, I'm not in the office much. Half of you think that I'm skiving, which is partly true, but that's not the full story. For the last six months, I've been checking out the competitive landscape and meeting with potential partners, suppliers and investors."

"So you've been skiving?" Flick asked.

Peter looked across at her, cautiously. "It's true that I take a lot of people out to dinner," he conceded. "But we think it's a worthwhile investment. Either way, it paid off. I can't give you the exact figures, but I can tell you that we're looking at an eight-figure investment from a coalition of venture capitalists. Shit just got real, guys. We're looking at one of the largest transatlantic tech deals in history. Let's get out there and show the rest of the world what we're made of."

***

John and Peter hadn't finished – far from it, in fact. But first, they had to deal with an unexpected backlash from the staff, starting with Flick.

"What about us?" she asked. "I don't know about everyone else, but I've invested time and money in this company. I'm not so sure about taking on extra investment. Do we really need it? Is it worth having some idiot in the Valley telling us what we can and can't do?"

"We thought about that," said John. "And we think we've come up with a solution."

"Good. Because if the deal's already signed, it's too late for you to change it."

"No one's changing anything," Peter said. "You'll still retain your shares, and they'll be worth even more by the time you sell them. Besides, we've cooked up a deal where John and I will retain full control of the company, so there's no need to worry about that. The contracts look legit, so take it easy and enjoy the ride."

"I'm not convinced," murmured Kerry, stroking the stubble on his chin. "And I don't like it."

"Understood," said John. "But sometimes there are things that we need you to trust us on. We can't tell you everything. In fact, the less we tell you, the better. Former.ly is built on secrecy."

"Just how many secrets are there?" I asked.

"Loads," Peter replied. "And we're about to tell you another one."

***

"As you might have noticed, Peter's been spending a lot of his time in Palo Alto," John said. "It's a techie's paradise over there. You can find anyone and everyone from coders and marketers to investors, advisors and specialists in start-up and immigration law."

"You can also find a lot of busboys and waitresses with broken dreams," Peter added. "But that's the nature of the business. You either make it or you don't. Everything else is just borrowed time."

"Thanks for that, Pete. Always the optimist," said John.

"Always the realist," he replied. "I'm just trying to prepare you guys for what's out there. Palo Alto is the city of broken dreams, but it's also the best place in the world to build a start-up."

"Exactly," said John. "And if it's the best place in the world to build a start-up, it's where we need to be. Ladies and gentlemen, pack your bags. Former.ly is moving stateside."

His announcement was met with stony silence. I don't know about the others, but I was busy thinking about the practicalities – the hows, the whens, and the whys. The two founders didn't seem surprised by the lacklustre response. Then again, John knew us better than our own mothers did, and Peter planned for everything. They already knew how we were going to react.

"Cheer up, guys," John laughed, breaking the stony silence. "It's like you didn't hear me. I said we're going to Palo Alto!"

"We heard you, John," Flick replied. We all watched her from the corners of our eyes, hardly daring to breathe. At times like these, Flick had an uncanny knack for picking up on the hidden thoughts of the rest of the group. "But this isn't the first time you've made a big decision without us, is it?"

"Flick, we're looking for loyalty here," John said. "We told you all when you joined that Former.ly would become your family. We'll take everyone who's willing to follow us. You can be sure of that. Peter's found a complex on the edge of town where we'll work, sleep and play. You went to university, Flick. Am I right?"

"Yes, Boss," she replied. "Graduated with honours."

"Then you know what to expect," John said. "We're chasing the same vibe. We're all in this together, folks."

"That's right," Peter added. "I can't wait for you guys to see it. It's got everything we'll ever need. There's even a gym, and we're throwing in food and accommodation."

"Sounds good to me," Kerry said. "But I'm an American. Of course I'm down with moving back to the States. What about the rest of the guys? They have families. What are they supposed to do?"

"We're your family now," John replied. "But if you can't come with us, then you'll have to stay behind. You're better off working for us than for one of our competitors, even if you are on the wrong side of the Atlantic."

"This is too much to take in," said Flick. "When's this all

happening, anyway?"

"I've already signed the lease," he told her. "We fly over as soon as we get our paperwork straight. Flick, you'll be working on that as of today. Start packing up your belongings and speak to Flick about it. She'll arrange for them to be shipped over."

"What happens to the people who stay behind?" Abhi asked.

John fixed his steely eyes on him and smiled. "We'll be keeping the London office open as well. Anyone who can't make the move to Palo Alto can stay here with Elaine. London will double as our financial HQ and our international meeting place, but Palo Alto is where the fun will be at. Any other questions?"

Abhi shook his head and a low murmur filled the air. John smiled and clapped his hands together. "Good!" he exclaimed. "Ladies and gentlemen, get ready. We're moving to California. Who's in?"

CHAPTER TWELVE

IT WAS THE FOLLOWING EVENING, and the Former.ly team was out for drinks at a cocktail bar in Covent Garden. There was standing room only by the time we arrived. Most people knocked off work while we were still sitting at our computer screens. Not that we were bothered. As long as the booze was flowing, we were happy.

Once every couple of months or so, we managed to talk John into releasing the credit card so that we could get loaded on company money. To us, it was one of the perks of the job. With no bill to worry about and a lot of steam to vent, those nights quickly got out of control. No one can party like a developer, especially when they're gearing up to move to Palo Alto.

"I can't wait to go," Flick shouted, struggling to make her voice heard over the din of the other pundits. "It's going to be like a holiday every day!"

"I don't know about that," I told her. "We'll still have to work, and we'll be living at the office too. There'll be no excuse not to work."

"So?" she said. "It worked for John and Peter. What are you afraid of?"

"I'm not afraid of anything. So you're in? You're up for the move?"

"Hell yeah," Flick replied. "I already spoke to my dad and he's cool with it. He says he'll come and stay once we've settled in, but I'm not so sure."

"What about your mum? What does she think?"

"Mum's dead, Dan. She died when I was little."

"Oh yeah," I said. "I forgot."

"Forget about it. We're here, and that's what matters. Anyway, let's change the subject. Abhi," she said, tapping the developer on the shoulder, "what about you?"

"What about me?" he replied.

Flick laughed. "Are you coming to Palo Alto?"

"I don't think so," he said. "It sounds like an adventure."

"And that's a problem?" I asked.

"Of course," he snapped. "I have a family to think about. What about my parents? My grandparents? Not to mention Sonal…"

"Who?" asked Flick, signalling to Peter across the bar and pointing to her empty glass. The founder nodded, grinned, and turned back to his conversation with John.

"Sonal's my wife," Abhi said. "I have a life. I have to provide for Sonal and our children. Our first one's on the way."

"So provide for them in Palo Alto," I said. "Bring 'em with you."

"No, sir," he replied. "A wife and kids locked up in Former.ly's new complex? No one wants that. Not them, not you, not anyone. Have you ever tried to code with a screaming baby in the room right next to you? Besides, Peter said we can stay here. We're keeping a skeleton staff in the UK, just in case."

"Just in case of what?"

"I guess we'll find out soon enough," he grumbled, draining his glass and setting it down on a nearby table. "I've got a bad feeling about this place. I'm going to get another drink."

***

From there, the night took a slow but inevitable turn for the worse. Now that Abhi had opened up, he didn't seem to care about what we thought of him. Now that Pandora's box was open, all bets were off. He was throwing back double Jägerbombs and leading the call for shots, and no one had the heart to argue with him.

Outside, over a cigarette that we shared despite neither of us being smokers, he told me his plan.

"I'm staying at Former.ly," he said. "Until the baby's born. Then I'm demanding paternity leave, and handing in my notice if the boys won't let me take it. Either way, I'm out of here, and they won't be able to do anything about it. They'll be on the other side of the ocean, and I'll be safe and sound with Sonal."

We finished the cigarette and headed back inside, where John was the centre of attention. "I think you're going to like the place that Peter found," he was saying. "It's awesome. We're moving to the best place in the world. It's going to be like living and working in a playground."

"I hate playgrounds," Kerry said, morosely. "Always have, even as a kid."

"That's 'cause you're too fat to fit on the swings," John laughed. "Don't worry, buddy. You're going to love this one."

"Don't you think it's going to be a little empty?" I asked. "How many of us will be living there?"

"A couple of dozen to begin with. But we're thinking big, Dan. We've quadrupled in size since you joined us, and we're getting bigger all the time. We don't want any of you to leave us, so we're going to make damn sure we keep you fed, housed and watered."

"You make it sound like a cult," I said. John looked at

me shrewdly through his beer goggles.

"Well, we are obsessed with death," he replied. "Besides, if we are a cult then it's your job to poison the Kool Aid."

"And it's my job to get people to drink it," Flick laughed.

After that, things got even hazier. I remember seeing Abhi with a drink in each hand and a cigarette in his mouth, and Peter almost got into a fistfight with an overexcited punter who called his bluff. John and I had to separate the two of them while Flick looked on and laughed. Josh, one of our juniors, threw up in the street and had to be sent home in the back of a taxi. Even Nils made an appearance.

"I'm only coming out for one," he'd said. He ended up staying out until two in the morning. Abhi was nowhere to be found, and Flick, John and Peter were in the middle of a heated discussion that I couldn't be bothered to get involved in. Kerry was at the bar with one of our junior developers, who'd put in a good effort despite arriving late. The two guys were chatting to a couple of women, the sort of girls who'd follow a guy to the bathroom for a double vodka and coke. I wanted no part in it.

The last thing I remember was catching Flick and Peter with their tongues down each other's throats on the dance floor. Realisation hit me, like the alcohol hit me every time I went outside for a breath of fresh air. I liked her. I liked her a lot. But I was pissed and pissed off, and she was all over Peter. I picked up my coat and walked out on to the street.

***

I woke up on the doorstep of John's flat; the silence of the night-struck city had been replaced by the singing of the birds and the hum of the commuter traffic. I was still drunk and I felt more tired than ever. From across the road, a young woman watched me from the corner of her eye as she climbed into her car. I struggled to breathe over the stench of my own sweat-stained clothing and wondered what the hell I was going to do next.

My watch read seven forty-five AM. I checked my pockets for my phone, my keys and my wallet, and I was relieved to find all three of them. I picked myself up from my perch, dusted myself down and headed towards the office. I expected to be the only one there, but I was wrong. I spotted the commotion as soon as I rounded the corner and began my final approach. Our parking spaces, which were usually empty because none of us could be bothered to drive, were unusually full. I spotted a couple of vans from regional news teams, and there was even a police car in a spot by the entrance.

"Excuse me," I said, pushing my way past a group of journalists in warm overcoats who were camping outside the entrance. One guy thrust a camcorder in my face and asked me for a comment and then cursed as I brushed his hand away and sent it clattering across the asphalt. Just as I thought he was about to take a swing at me, Nils surfaced and escorted me inside.

I knew something was wrong immediately. The office was in disarray, and Flick was sobbing at her desk. Kerry was there too, looking worried and sipping absently at a cup of coffee. John was in the boardroom. I could see him through the glass, talking to a pair of uniformed policemen. There was no sign of the rest of the team.

"Kerry, what's going on?" I asked.

He looked up at me, slowly. "Didn't you hear the news? It's Abhi. He's dead."

CHAPTER THIRTEEN

IT WAS FOUR HOURS LATER, and I'd sobered up dramatically and settled into the beginning of a two-day hangover. John and Peter announced a day of mourning and allowed us all to go home, but most of us stayed in the office anyway. None of us had anywhere to go, and Former.ly was our family. We'd lost one of our own.

John spent most of the morning in the boardroom with the police officers, and we watched the proceedings with a morbid interest, too distraught to do anything other than to think of our dead friend, a guy who'd been so alive and full of life just twenty-four hours earlier. Nothing could lighten the mood. Even Flick couldn't break the tension.

Peter arrived at the office at about quarter to one. "It's crazy out there," he told us. "Fucking vultures."

"They're still gathering, then?" It was a stupid question to ask. We could still hear them baying at our doors and blockading us in the office. One guy tried to climb in through a first floor window. Luckily, Flick was looking out of it at the time, and she slammed it closed just as he was pulling level. He lost his footing and fell to the floor. Peter didn't care, but Flick nearly lost her mind. She sighed with relief when he got back up again. We'd had enough bad news for the day.

"Of course they're still gathering," Peter snapped. "We haven't released a statement yet, and their papers won't sell themselves. But what the hell are we supposed to say?

Besides, we need John to sign it off. Where the hell is he, anyway?"

"In the boardroom with the feds," said Kerry. "Where have you been?"

"Me? I had a couple of things to sort out," he replied. "Thank God for Nils and his men. I wouldn't have made it up here without them. Those journalists were pressing in from all angles."

"How many are there?" I asked.

"Must be a couple of dozen of journos, plus maybe half a dozen policemen. We're going international, folks. I spotted CNN, the BBC and Reuters. Forget about the tech press."

"Shit," said Kerry. "So what are we going to do?"

"We're going to do what we do best," Peter replied. "We're going to strengthen our servers and try to weather out the storm. There's nothing else we can do."

"But what about Abhi?"

"What about him?" Peter sighed. "Abhi's dead. It's harsh, but it's true. What do you want me to do about it? Do you want me to bring him back? My job is to make sure that Former.ly doesn't die with him."

"You're a heartless bastard," said Flick, with tears flowing from her eyes again. She didn't cry often, but now that she'd opened the floodgates it all started pouring out of her. "He was a good friend to me – to all of us."

I pulled my hood up and turned away, so that my face was hidden. Truth was, I was tearing up as well, and I didn't want anyone else to see it. There was no time for weakness at Former.ly. Abhi hadn't exactly been a brother to me, but he'd been somewhere between a friend and an acquaintance, and I'd grown to like him, in a way. Things wouldn't be the same without him.

"I'm just doing my job," Peter replied. "Perhaps it's time you did yours, Flick. You're in charge of our public image, so take charge. What are you going to do about this mess?"

Flick said nothing. She just flushed and leaned back in her chair as if she'd been slapped. Silence descended upon us like a dark cloud, and we all sat back in our own little worlds, just waiting for the police to leave and for John to tell us what the hell was going on.

***

When John escorted the policemen to the door, all eyes were on him. Our uneasy silence had continued even after Flick put the radio on. We listened to it for twenty minutes or so and then turned it off again when the news came on, in case we were on it.

"Well thank you for your time, Mr. Mayers," one of the officers was saying. "We'll be back in touch if we have any further questions."

"I look forward to it," John replied. "Now if you don't mind, I've got a business to run. Do let me know if we can help any further with your investigation."

The officer scowled at him and said, "I'd like to speak to the rest of your team. Seems to me that there's a lot of death around these parts. Now, you lot being the law-abiding gentlemen that you are, I'm sure that none of you have anything to do with it. But let's suppose that one of your employees happened to know something – some minor detail, perhaps something that they don't even know that they know about. Wouldn't you want us to know so that we can find your colleague's killer?"

John reluctantly complied and introduced the officer to the team. "Do what you've got to do. Folks, you're going to have to talk to the police." He sighed and pinched the bridge of his nose. "Flick," he said, "get me a cup of coffee, love. I need it."

"Sure thing, Boss."

While she was gone, the police officer started searching for a convenient place to interview the Former.ly team, and John started his story. "I'm sure you've all heard the bad news by now. Abhi is dead. We've lost one of our own. This is a sad day for Former.ly. But that's not all there is to it. Foul play is suspected. He was found floating in the Thames this morning."

"Christ," I said. "That's terrible. What happened?"

"Apparently the cops aren't sure. They'll need to wait for the autopsy to know for certain, but I'm guessing it's nothing obvious like a gunshot or a stabbing. Hell, he could have fallen into the river on his stumble home."

"He wouldn't have been walking home," I told him. "Not Abhi, not in the middle of the night. He lived in Hammersmith. That's a hell of a long way to walk."

"You're right," he replied. "But it's not up to us to figure that out. That's what we have a police force for. They spoke to me about his final movements. I'll be honest, last night is a little hazy, but I told them everything I could. Hell, I've got nothing to hide. Now it's your turn to do the same. No big deal."

***

"Let's make a vow." It was three o'clock in the afternoon, and the Former.ly team was gathered around the boardroom table for an impromptu meeting. John was chairing the proceedings, and it was John who was doing the talking. "Maybe a vow isn't the right word for it, but I can't think of anything better. I want us all to fess up to what we were doing last night, just so there's no confusion or suspicion."

"You think it might have been someone at the company,

Boss?" Flick asked.

"That, Flick, is exactly what I'm trying to avoid. I don't think it was anyone here, but I do think he died because of Former.ly. Perhaps it was a robbery gone wrong, or maybe they wanted information and he wouldn't give it to them. The office has been attacked before, so who's to say that our assailants, whoever the hell they are, haven't stepped up their game?"

"Do you think we're in danger?" I asked.

"Truthfully, yes," John replied. "But we'll be safe in Palo Alto, and that's one of the reasons why we've taken on the complex. We're stronger when we're together. And we're stronger when we trust each other, which is why I want the truth from you all."

"Do we really have to do this?" Kerry grumbled.

"We really have to do this," he said. "But if it helps, I'll go first. I was here at the office. Call me crazy, but I had a feeling something bad was going to happen, so I came back to look things over and to get a few things done. Waste of time, really. I had to check over it all in the morning anyway."

"And can anyone prove that?" Nils asked.

"Check the CCTV," John replied. "That'll back me up. So what about you, Dan? Where were you?"

Cursing inwardly, but with little choice, I recounted my drunken wanderings in as much detail as I could remember. I said that I was also on CCTV and that if anyone wanted to check my alibi, they'd have to involve the cops.

"I guess I'll go next," said Kerry, shifting position uncomfortably. "When I left the club, I went home to bed. Looks like my life is pretty boring. No alibis, guys. I sleep alone."

"Speak for yourself," Peter said. "Did anyone see you? A neighbour? A doorman?"

"No one," Kerry replied.

"It's not like you to skip on a takeaway, Kerry," Peter laughed. "Well, I guess it's my turn. I was back at John's place with company. I didn't get her name, but if I've still got her number I can try to track her down, if you want."

"That won't be necessary," John replied. "Just make sure you change the bed sheets. What about you, Flick. Where were you last night?"

"I…," she faltered. It took her a second to pull her thoughts together. "I don't remember. I remember being at the club, and then somewhere else after that. Somewhere dark and quiet. I woke up this morning in the hallway outside my apartment. I guess I left my keys here. Had to walk in, in my high heels."

***

The rest of the team shared where they were, but nothing came to light and John ordered us to get back to work as if nothing had happened. By the time I left the office, the fury of the press was reaching fever pitch. The world's journalists were gathered on our doorstep, and #Formerly was trending worldwide across multiple social networks, our own included.

"I'm just glad our servers can take the hammering," Peter said. "Let me tell you guys a little secret. We've partnered with some good friends of mine to make sure that we're covered all over the world. We're particularly strong in America and the U.K. You're never more than eighty miles away from one of our servers, unless you're in Alaska. And, let's face it, no one's ever in Alaska."

Things were so bad outside that Nils and his men had stopped trying to keep the entrance clear and had retreated to the inside of the building. They were keeping people out, but we couldn't exactly nip out for a pint of milk. I left under cover of darkness and descended the fire escape to try to avoid the milling crowds, but there were still a half-dozen journalists lurking around the back of the building. Two of them were smoking cigarettes, and they were talking to an elderly Indian woman who looked familiar, somehow.

I tried to sneak past them while their attention was distracted, but they turned to look at me. Before I knew what was happening, the woman was on me like a police dog at the heels of a criminal. The reporters followed the two of us down the street in a bizarre conga line as she shouted at me for something that wasn't my fault.

"You," she yelled, jabbing a finger at me. "You work for that terrible company. It's your fault that my son is dead!"

"You must be Abhi's mother," I said, still walking towards the Tube station. "Mrs. Desi, I'm so sorry for your loss. Your son was a good friend of mine, and I know I speak on behalf of the rest of the team when I say he'll be sorely missed."

"That means nothing to me," she growled. "You can't bring my son back. Nobody can. He's dead. He's gone for good. Your company took him away from us, and now I have to bury my son before my husband. My grandson will grow up without a father. Who killed him? Which one of you murdered my son?"

"Mrs. Desi," I replied, stopping suddenly and spinning around to give her my full attention. "Look, we're all as upset as you are. I can assure you that if we knew anything at all about what happened to your son, we'd tell the police. Take my advice and let them do their job. If anyone can find out what happened, they can."

"Look me in the eye and tell me that you know nothing about what happened," she screamed. The reporters lurking in the background were now catching the whole affair on video. I looked her in the eye.

"I swear to you, if I could help you then I would. Nobody's more upset than I am, but there's nothing that I can do, and nothing that Former.ly can do either."

"How dare you?" With a surprising strength, she spread her fingers and slapped me across the face. She hit me so hard that I still had white lines on my cheek in the morning. I heard the clicking of the journalists' cameras and felt my heart sink in the sure knowledge that the confrontation would be shown in papers across the world.

"Mrs. Desi," I replied, trying to stay calm in the face of insanity. "I'm sorry, I didn't mean to offend you. It's been a long day and I need some sleep."

Her expression seemed to soften, but only a little. Her eyes were just as sharp and mournful as before. "It has," she agreed. "And I'm sorry too."

***

I should've known that the drama wasn't over. In my life, nothing's ever that simple. It was dark by the time I got home, and my head was ringing with the tinnitus you get when you drink too much and don't get any sleep. I just wanted to climb into bed and to sleep until the next millennium. Unfortunately, Sarah had other plans.

She was sitting cross-legged in the living room when I arrived. I knew something was wrong by the look in her eye, and by the way that she flinched when I walked over to hug her.

"Dan," she said, "we need to talk."

"That never sounds good," I replied. "What do we need to talk about?"

Sarah sighed. "It's about us, Dan. I can't do it anymore. I don't love you, and I don't think that you love me. If you do, you're doing a bad job of showing it."

I thought about protesting, but she had a point. I didn't know what to say, so I waited for her to continue.

"The thing is, Dan, we're growing apart. More than that, we've already grown apart. You've got your life and I've got mine. It's crunch time. I can't put my career on hold to move to America with you, and you can't put your career on hold to stay."

I nodded. "I'd thought the same thing myself," I admitted. "Only I guess I've been too scared to say so."

This time, Sarah nodded. She had tears in her eyes, but they were old tears, like she'd got her crying out of the way beforehand so she could maintain her composure. "Thanks, Dan," she said. "For being a grown-up."

"Don't mention it," I murmured. My stomach churned and bubbled over as I wondered whether we were making the right decision, but then I realised something. It was the only decision to make. "So what happens next?"

"I'm not sure," Sarah admitted. "I guess we'll figure it out as we go along. But we need to take this seriously, Dan. One of us is going to have to move out of here, the sooner the better."

"I'll do it," I said. "I'll be out of your way by the end of the week."

CHAPTER FOURTEEN

IN THE END, I sought help from the only person I could think of. Flick let me crash at her place. I slept on the sofa, much to the annoyance of her flatmate, a woman called Helen who occasionally wandered in for a glass of water in the middle of the night.

When I explained what had happened, Flick showed no sign of surprise, but then she already knew my relationship's troubled history. In fact, she'd given me advice before, whether I'd asked for it or not. She'd even promised me a place to stay if everything went wrong. I guess it was time for her to make good on that promise.

"You can stay here as long as you want," she told me. "I spoke to Helen and she's fine with you staying on the sofa as long as you help with the housework and chip in for the rent."

"Thanks," I said. "That means a lot. I could use a place to hang my hat right now."

"You'll have to find somewhere for your stuff, though. You're not going to be able to bring it all here. This is a temporary solution, not a new home."

"I'll put it into storage," I promised. "It'll only need to stay there for a couple of weeks, and then I can have it forwarded to Palo Alto."

"Dan," she said, clasping my hand in hers, "you can talk to me about anything. You know that, right? I'm on your side."

"I know," I said.

I leant in slowly and kissed her on her soft, gentle lips. She kissed me back and my heart raced with endorphins. Then, we broke off the kiss, and the moment was gone.

"We should go to work," she said.

***

When we both arrived at the office, John told us that Peter had jetted off to Palo Alto. "He's gone to meet with our investors again," he said. "There are some papers to sign. He's also got some stuff to sort out at the new facility. Besides, we need to do some work on the servers, and we don't trust anyone else to do it."

"What sort of work?" I asked. John looked directly at me, his shrewd eyes boring into mine as though he was reading the schema on the back of my skull. Then, he chuckled, softly.

"If I told you that, I'd have to kill you," he replied. "We're taking no chances with this one, Dan."

I caught up with Flick over a cup of coffee. We snuck off to Starbucks, claiming our right to a rare lunch break. Kerry stared at us as we left the office together, and I could see his crazy brain trying to work out what was going on. Still, despite our hurried kiss that morning, there was nothing between us other than the shared relationship of two colleagues at a frenetic internet start-up.

We sat down at a table and nursed our coffees for several minutes. Then, Flick broke the silence. "I think something strange is going on," she said. "Don't ask me why, but I'm getting bad vibes from the boys."

"I know what you mean," I told her. "But I wouldn't admit it in front of them. I don't trust anyone."

"Not even me?"

"Not even you," I laughed. "But whatever's going on, I intend to find out."

"Oh yeah?" she said. "Can I help?"

"You serious?" I asked. "You realise that we don't even know what we're looking for, right? We're fighting a war against shadows."

Flick nodded. "I just want the truth," she said. "For Abhi's sake. He shouldn't have died. If we were attacked by some unknown adversary, they should've killed John or Peter instead."

"They shouldn't have killed anyone," I replied. "I didn't sign up for this shit."

"Me neither. But we're here now, and we've got to make the best of it. We've got to find out what's going on or die trying. We need to do it for Abhi."

"And for Mrs. Desi," I added. "And Sonal, and for the kid who'll grow up without a father."

"Exactly," said Flick. "Justice must be done."

***

That evening, when Flick and I were back at her place watching reruns of *Friends* and eating popcorn on the sofa, she took a phone call from John. She disappeared into her bedroom, so I stretched out on the sofa with the remote and started flicking through the channels. Nothing on, as usual.

Flick emerged ten minutes later with the residue of tears around her eyes. "That bastard," she said, flopping down beside me. "He wants me to go into the office. It's ten o'clock at night!"

"What does he need you for?" I asked. "It's a bit late to call you in."

"That's what I said. In the end, he said I could stay here

if I get some work done. And let me tell you, some serious work needs doing."

"Why?" I asked. "What happened?"

"The servers are down again," she grimaced. "Peter called in from Cali. He's in a rage. The site is down across the globe. Even our backup servers can't take the strain. He's been trying to get third-parties involved to take over any excess, but no one wants to handle our data."

"In some ways, I'm not surprised," I said. "We're hot stuff at the moment. No wonder our servers are taking a kicking."

Flick sighed, grabbed her laptop and started tapping away at the keyboard. There was still nothing on TV, so I put *Friends* back on and grabbed my own machine. I was inundated with e-mails as soon as I turned it on. I sighed and began to work my way through them in an act of solidarity. It's the Former.ly way – if one of us is working, we all work.

Flick's housemate came in a couple of hours later. She'd picked up a guy on a night out and brought him back home. Unfortunately for her, we were still up at two in the morning. The site was back online and Flick was working furiously to put out fires, the sweat dripping from her forehead. Calls to the office were being routed to her mobile phone, and it ended up buzzing so often that she had to turn it off before we both went crazy.

"Oh hey, Flick," Helen said, standing awkwardly by the door to her room. "I thought you guys would be asleep by now. Don't you have work in the morning?"

"What the fuck do you think we're doing right now?" growled Flick.

***

I didn't get much sleep that evening. Flick was working until an ungodly hour. Even though I slept for a while, curled up with her on the sofa with my head on her shoulder while she pounded the keys on her laptop, it wasn't true sleep, the kind of sleep that you get on a comfortable bed in a quiet room when you don't have to get up in the morning.

At the office the following day, you could tell that no one had slept. John looked utterly exhausted with dark sacks around his eyes and an uncontrollable shake, like a man who'd had too much caffeine. Even Kerry looked tired, despite the fact that he had nothing to do with the infrastructure. My guess was that he'd been up late playing Call of Duty with his friends back in America. Only the juniors looked fresh, and that didn't last for long. John was in a foul temper, and he ordered them around like a madman.

"Go easy on them, John," I said, pulling him aside in the kitchen. "The last thing we need now is a mistake. You're giving them more than they can handle. Hell, even if they all stayed here until midnight, they wouldn't get it done. You're forgetting that we don't have Abhi anymore."

"I'm very much aware of our resources, Dan. Don't try to tell me how to do my job. Why don't you focus on your own work instead of worrying about everyone else?"

"You're the boss," I replied, reluctantly. Truth be told, I was ahead of schedule. We were rolling out new functionality, a way to monetise our users by allowing them to buy virtual wreathes and artefacts, and most of my work was already done. I was waiting for Kerry to finish off the visuals so I could code them in and launch an alpha. As usual, he was taking his time.

I tried to keep myself busy by cracking on with bug fixes and catching up with e-mails, but I'd gotten so much done the night before that I ran out of work by lunchtime, and

Kerry said his renders wouldn't be ready until three o'clock. Flick was still busy dealing with the fallout from the server collapse, so I couldn't even sneak out for a drink with her.

In the end, I booted up my journal and started to write. I hadn't updated it for a couple of weeks, and I didn't feel much like writing in it at Flick's place. Nothing says antisocial like typing in your journal when someone's sitting beside you and trying to talk to you. That said, trying to write at work was just as difficult, and I couldn't shake the feeling that someone was watching me.

I looked up from my screen and saw John's piercing eyes locked in my direction. I gave him a swift thumbs-up (which he failed to return) and then closed my journal and surfed the web at random until Kerry's files were ready.

***

John went out to get coffee. When he got back he went into a side room for a debriefing with Nils. When he came back out again, his face was the colour of a radish, and he called a quick team meeting to share the news.

"Okay, folks," he said, clapping his hands together. "Listen up. Now, as you know, we've been working with Nils and his security firm to make things safer around here. We don't want any work-related accidents now, do we?"

"You mean like what happened to Abhi?" Flick murmured. I ignored her.

"So here's the deal," John continued. "Nils and his men have been working hard to keep the office safe, and we've stepped up security inside and out. But protecting ourselves isn't enough. We need to get out there and go on the offensive, which is why I asked Nils to look into who it is that's been trying to break into our offices."

"And did you find anything out?" I asked.

John grinned. "Of course, I did. You still with that woman of yours, Dan?"

"Sarah?" I asked. "No. We went our separate ways."

"Good," John replied, the smile vanishing from his face to be replaced by a look of sincerity. "Make sure it stays that way. Those goons who keep trying to break into the office. We managed to track them back to TheNextWeb – hired on the orders of Alex, their editor."

"You mean the guy that died?"

"The very same," John said. "I guess his shady dealings came back to haunt him."

Flick shuddered. "Shouldn't we go to the police?" she asked.

John spun around to look at her. "Hell no," he scowled. "Let them figure that out by themselves. The good news is they won't be coming back any time soon. But if you tell the cops about this, then they're going to start asking more questions. I don't like questions. So don't ask any more. Get back to work, folks. There's a lot for us to do."

***

It was several weeks later, and our move to Palo Alto was imminent. John was in the best mood I'd seen him in for months, probably because the media shitstorm had finally died down after Abhi's final send-off at a quiet ceremony in North London. The press weren't invited and neither were we, which didn't surprise us. We memorialised him with a wake of our own in the office. John also agreed to use his name for one of the new variables that we were coding into the system. There were plenty of tears when the code went live – one last reminder that he'd never again saunter into the office with his mother's laal maans.

I was sitting with Flick and Kerry at the table in the

kitchen when John came in with a tray of coffee and a huge smile on his face. He handed out the coffee and told us to head to the boardroom for a surprise announcement.

Five minutes later, the entire company was gathered around the boardroom table. John entered last and closed the door behind him. It was hot – too hot – and the stifling air clawed at my throat and nostrils. I opened a window to let some air in, but the roar of traffic drifted in with the breeze and John told me to close it again. I reluctantly did as I was told.

"Okay, listen up," said John, clapping his hands together and jerking me out of my reverie. "Now that we're all here, are you ready to hear the news?" We all grunted in agreement, like an unruly class of schoolchildren complying with a supply teacher. "Good," he continued. "Now, as you all already know, we're moving to Palo Alto in just under a month.

"Now, unfortunately, not everyone is going to be able to make it. Elaine here is going to stay behind to turn this place into our accounts office, and to make sure we have a base whenever we're travelling. We might even hire further staff over here to turn it into a secondary office, but make no mistake about it – our new home is Palo Alto.

"Former.ly is going places, ladies and gentlemen, as the latest figures show. Time on site is up, sign-ups are growing month-on-month, and we're serving more visitors than ever. But that's not all. We've launched dozens of new features since our beta, and we're about to release one of the most important updates in the company's history. Dan, why don't you tell us all about it?"

"There's not much to say, really," I said. "We're looking to monetise our visitors and to show our investors that the site could become a cash cow, so we're launching the ability for people to purchase virtual gifts to leave on the pages of dead friends and relatives."

"That's the plan," said John. "Right now, we have twenty-five million active users and over nineteen thousand deaths. Those stats might sound impressive, but they're still on the rise and we're on course to double that in less than a year. I'll be circulating some usage goals before the end of the week, and Peter and I want you to work towards them. Former.ly is a team effort, and we need your help if we're going to take over the world. Who's with me?"

CHAPTER FIFTEEN

THE MOVING DATE edged closer, and the office looked even more like a shit-heap than usual. Most of the fixtures and fittings had been stripped from the walls and packed into boxes, surrounded by styrofoam and wrapped with heavy duty masking tape. Flick's desk had been disassembled, and so had several of the others. Meanwhile, John had called in the decorators to try to spruce the place up. I had no idea what they were doing, but half of the office was covered with sheets and the other half was piled high with ladders, buckets, paintbrushes and overalls.

"Dan," scowled John, storming over as soon as I walked through the door. "Where've you been? You're late." I checked my phone and glared back at him.

"Sorry, Boss," I replied, even though I wasn't. "What's new?"

"Oh, not much, you know. Just the biggest shitstorm to hit the site since we started, and Flick's not here to deal with it. I can't even get hold of her on the phone. Her number's engaged. Must be those bloody journalists chasing her for a quote. Vultures, the lot of them. If she's smart, she'll say nothing until she speaks to me. I hope to God she's smart."

"She'll be fine," I told him. "She's not stupid. What happened, anyway?"

"Same thing that always happens," he grumbled. "Someone posted a story without checking their facts or their priorities. Now it seems like everyone under the sun is after our blood, and don't get me started on the bloggers. Turns out that providing a service isn't good enough, and now people are questioning how we use their data."

"And how do we use it?" I asked. In my entire time at the company, no one had ever explained it to me.

"Forget about it," he told me. "Some things are better left alone." He patted me on the shoulder and walked away, leaving me confused and on my own in the middle of the office.

***

I passed out at my desk and got woken up the following morning by the buzzer, which was ringing repeatedly and thwarting my efforts to nod back off. I glanced at my phone and took in the time (quarter to seven) and the flood of notifications that had flooded in overnight. I groaned and got ready for work.

It was too early in the morning for surprises, but I had one anyway – two parked police cars outside the office, and four policemen perched impatiently beside the buzzer. One of Nils's men let them in reluctantly, after thoroughly inspecting their IDs.

"Don't mind us," said one of the policeman, the guy who seemed to be in charge of the operation. "We're just doing our jobs."

"Yeah," the security guard replied. "And so am I. But you're not the one who has to tell John Mayers that you let the police into his office while he wasn't there."

***

John was pissed off; no, more than that – he was livid. When I got hold of him to tell him what had happened, he virtually exploded down the handset, shrieking and cursing and threatening to take my job. I knew he'd regret it and apologise later – he needs me and I know too much – but that didn't make it any easier. Eventually, he put the phone down. He was in the office less than ten minutes later.

"John," Nils said, laying a hand on him as he entered the building. "I'm sorry. It's not like they gave me any choice. They're the police, John. What else was I supposed to do?" It was the first time I'd ever heard Nils sound scared, almost apologetic.

"Forget about it," he snapped. "You've done enough."

He shook free of Nils and stormed into the kitchen where England's finest were relaxing with the tea that I'd offered them, trying to stall them as much as possible while I waited for reinforcements. John greeted them with a scowl and led them silently through to the boardroom. Ten minutes later, Kerry and Nils crossed the threshold, and I was no longer alone inside the office.

"What's going on?" Kerry asked.

I shrugged. "Oh, the usual. The police are here. John took them through to the boardroom."

"What's it all about?"

"I have no idea," I replied. "But I have a feeling we're about to find out."

Right on cue, the boardroom door opened and John led the policemen out. "So if you'll excuse me," he was saying, as he attempted to usher them towards the door, "I'm a busy man, and I'm sure you're busy men too. I'll take up no more of your valuable time."

Outside the building, one of the officers paused and took John aside. "We're not finished with you, Mr. Mayers," he said. "Don't forget. We have access to the results of the autopsy. In most cases, the victim and the murderer know each other, and it seems to me that no one knew him better than you and your employees. If one of you did it, we'll find out. And if you weren't responsible, you could all be in danger. Could be that the assailant targeted him because he worked for you."

"Thanks for your warning," John said. "But I think we'll take our chances. Was there anything else that you wanted?"

"I think that's about it," the officer said. "Oh, and my name's Whitehouse. Sam Whitehouse. Here, take my card. You might need it someday."

***

Two days later, I climbed into a cab with Flick and we headed to the airport. There was a hum of excitement in the air. Some of us – Kerry in particular – had no idea if we'd ever come back. For Kerry, the move to Palo Alto was a triumphant return to his homeland, despite the fact that he grew up in Iowa. Palo Alto was almost as alien to him as it was to us.

"Is everyone here?" John asked, looking around at his employees.

The team looked around uneasily. I started to wonder what I was doing and whether I'd made the right decision. I'd grown up in London, and I'd spent most of my life in the city. I'd never been to America, not even for a holiday. I saw the same tension in the faces of my colleagues – only Peter, John and Kerry seemed immune.

I felt uneasy for a different reason. I missed Abhi. Although I'd always known that he'd be staying behind, I didn't expect him to be staying behind in a coffin. At that moment, I would have given anything just to hear his voice again, to talk about variables and new programming languages and to joke about the new responsibilities he'd have to take on when his firstborn arrived.

We had plenty of time left over, but John still hurried us towards check-in as though he expected something to go wrong. He was right to worry; as we headed towards the desk, we were stopped in our tracks by a familiar face – the police officer from earlier that week, now out of uniform and without the backup of his buddies.

"Going somewhere, gentlemen?" he asked.

John laughed, a hoot of defiance that made passers-by turn their heads to look at him as they pushed their suitcases towards the check-in desk. "Why certainly, Officer," he replied. "Haven't you seen the news? We're a big deal on the internet. We're relocating to the States, is that a crime?"

"Relocating isn't," the policeman replied. "But murder is. We have nothing on you or your team. At least, not yet. Without sufficient evidence, I can't hold you here. You're free to do as you please, but if I find something – anything – then I'll be seeing you again. Be careful, Mr. Mayers. The truth will out."

John's smile faded as rapidly as it had appeared. He turned abruptly on his heels and marched towards the check-in desk. The rest of us followed him into uncertainty. Into Former.ly's future.

To Palo Alto.

CHAPTER SIXTEEN

THE SUN WAS SETTING in California as we disembarked the aeroplane and headed through the terminus. I could already feel the difference, a subtle change in the atmosphere and a total change of temperature along with a slight sweetness to the air that spoke of a completely different ecosystem.

The two founders pulled out all the stops for our arrival. A minibus showed up to collect our luggage, but we were bundled into the backs of limousines. John helped himself to a bottle of bubbly from the minibar, which he cracked open and poured into flutes. Then, Kerry made the mistake of switching on the TV, and John's mood went downhill immediately. Local news channels were reporting on our arrival, recycling a grainy shot of the team as we walked across the precinct of San Jose International Airport.

"Former.ly is a British success story," the reporter was saying. I doubt he'd even heard of us before we showed up at the airport. "Shaking off controversy, they've made the journey across the Atlantic to become the latest start-up to call Palo Alto home. Early reports suggest…"

"Turn that rubbish off!" John bellowed. Kerry was so stunned by the sudden outburst that he dropped the remote, and I had to pick it up and do the job for him. "They're after our blood already, and we've only just landed."

"How did they even know we were here?" one of the juniors asked, staring in awe at the screen. "Do you think they have someone on the inside?"

"Why?" John scowled. "Have you got something you want to tell us? Besides, it's not like we're coming here in secret. Sure, we might not be making a song and dance about it, but it's all over the internet if you know where to look. Let's just keep our heads down until we make it to the compound, okay? Now pass me another bottle. We're supposed to be celebrating."

✦✦✦

The paparazzi greeted us at the gates to Former.ly's new office, but John and Peter were well-prepared. When John called it a compound, he hadn't been joking. We passed through two security checkpoints that were patrolled by butch-looking Americans with a motley assortment of crew cuts, tattoos and piercings. The outer perimeter surrounded the car park, and the press had slipped through it with the persistence and inevitable momentum of waves crashing against the shore.

The second perimeter was a different matter entirely. Even to my untrained eye, it was clearly a newer addition, an eight-foot electric fence with barbed wire and anti-vandal paint. The cast iron gates looked solid and imposing, and they swung open electronically when the driver of the limo wound down the window and flashed his ID at the scanner. A half-dozen opportunistic journos tried to squeeze through with the limo, only to be pushed back by a couple of security guards with fierce-looking Alsatians whose job was to patrol the fence's perimeter and to scare the crap out of anyone who tried to get through. I raised an eyebrow at John and he laughed.

"What?" he said. "You can't blame us for being security conscious, especially after what that cop said back at the airport. Ah, America! The best place in the world to start your own army without breaking the law."

"And who's paying for all of this?"

"Our investors," John replied. "And eventually, our users."

The driver parked the limo right outside the building, and the Former.ly team stepped unsteadily out on to the warm Californian asphalt. Dusk had settled in and night was on its way, but the air was disconcertingly warm and the humidity left us clawing at our collars. I've never liked wearing shorts, but I soon got used to it in Palo Alto.

None of us knew what to expect from the office, but the outside made me think of a concentration camp. That couldn't have been further from the truth. It was a paradise, a playground for grown-ups and the perfect place to live, work and play. I suspected it was all part of the plan. The drab exterior and the comfortable interior made sure that no one would ever want to leave.

Even from just inside the entrance, we got a good view of the place. Desks made from Lego blocks were scattered across the floor, separated by pool tables and a jukebox. I could even see an electric guitar and an amplifier, despite the fact that none of us could play. The walls and ceilings were painted in garish colours that reflected the light from the huge chandeliers and the wide bay windows.

In their typically idiosyncratic style, the founders had thought about transportation too. Peter rolled up to greet us on the back of a Segway.

"What up, guys?" he said. "And welcome to Former.ly, Palo Alto! Come on. Let me show you to your rooms."

***

We followed Peter as he led us through the office,

weaving in and out of the desks on his Segway until we reached a large set of double doors, right beside a breakout area with a couple of sofas, a television and a games console.

"This is the kitchen," he announced, hopping off the Segway and leaning it against the wall. "Help yourselves to anything you find in here. It's all paid for by the company."

As he spoke, he pushed open the doors and led the way into a large, freshly fitted kitchen. Peter smiled at our awestruck expressions and began to wander around the room, opening cupboards at random to show off the produce and equipment inside them.

"Of course," he continued, "you're free to get your own food too. Just make sure you initial it so that the rest of us know not to eat it. If you've got any requests, then send them through to Pam. She's our new office manager, and she'll be keeping us stocked up."

"And what about the cleaning?" asked Kerry. "Someone's got to do it."

"Don't worry," Peter replied. "We've got a cleaner. A guy called Nate. You'll get to meet him at some point. He's coming round twice a week to handle the communal areas, so you only need to worry about your rooms. Speaking of which, let's go. The tour's not over yet, folks."

***

Peter continued to lead the way with John a couple of steps behind him. A rear entrance to the kitchen led into a bizarre internal garden, which was surrounded by the walls of the complex. The building looked like a doughnut from the air, a doughnut surrounded by the fence of death.

"The halls are just through here," said Peter, leading the way along a walkway. "And don't forget, we've also got a gymnasium and a common room with an HD TV where

Kerry can show off his movies."

"Woohoo!" he cheered. "It's about damn time."

"Quite," said John. "But it's for work as well as play, so don't get carried away. We've got a job to do, after all."

Peter continued to lead the way, back into the complex and up a narrow flight of stairs. It reminded me of being back at university, only the rooms were smaller and the office was our common room. Without our belongings, the rooms looked bare and empty, but I guessed that they'd look comfortable enough in time. Besides, it wasn't like we'd spend much time in them, other than when we were sleeping.

"So that's it, folks," said John, taking over the role as our tour guide. "We'll go grab a cup of tea and figure out who's staying where, and then we'll hand over your keys. Any questions?"

"Yeah," Kerry said. "I have a question. Where do you guys keep the beer?"

CHAPTER SEVENTEEN

WE SETTLED into American life pretty quickly, although my dire predictions came true. We had almost no time to ourselves, and we got used to treating the office like a giant common room. It didn't matter what the time was, you could always guarantee that at least two people were working and at least two more were kicking back and relaxing. With Former.ly, it was often difficult to tell the difference between the two. Flick was the only one of us who stuck to her contractual hours, mainly because she had to. Our users were online around the clock and so were our developers, but Flick only had to worry about the press.

One Tuesday afternoon, a couple of weeks after we moved into the complex, Peter rolled into the office on his Segway and called an emergency meeting at the bar, which had become our go-to place for everything from weekly kick-offs to brainstorms and corporate announcements. One thing was for sure – something interesting always happened when we gathered there, even if it was just Kerry lining up a row of shots and then spewing them back up onto his shoes. On this day, though, Peter had something on his mind.

"Well, folks," he said. "Thanks for giving me some time. I know we're pretty short on that at the moment, so I'll keep this brief. Former.ly has been nominated for an award. We're up for the Best New Start-up at TechCrunch Disrupt, and John and I have been nominated for Founders of the Year. How about that?"

"That's awesome," said Flick, leaning in for a high-five. "I'll get on it straight away. At last, something to shout about!"

"No, you won't," Peter replied. "At least, not yet. First, we need to win the damn thing."

"But what if we don't win it?"

"Of course, we'll win it. We're Former.ly. In fact, that's something else we need to talk about. We need to sort out numbers for the ceremony. I want us to have a decent presence there when we win it. John's going to work on our acceptance speech, and I'll be sorting out travel and accommodation. We don't need the whole team to go – just the best of the best."

"Oh yeah?" I laughed. "And who are our best?"

"Well, you're one of them," Peter said. "And we'll take Flick and Kerry along too. John, Nils and I will be going, but we need a couple more to fill the table. That's where the fun comes in. John, want to tell them your idea?"

"Sure thing," he said. "Peter and I have figured out a fair way to decide who gets the seats. We're going to have a pitch day on Monday. If you want to join us in New York, you need to tell us why you deserve to go. Peter and I will listen to the pitches and allocate the remaining seats from there. Any questions? No? Good. Then get back to work."

***

On the day of the pitches, we ordered in some pizza and cracked open a couple of beers. It was a long and boring day. Some of our newbies were fired up with excitement, but I had the cynicism of an old-timer. The whole thing was just a charade, a popularity contest that I wanted no part in.

Luckily, I blagged my way out of it by faking a setback in the new internal ranking system. The plan was to show users how active they'd been and how many words they'd posted on the site. It could either encourage them or deter them, and we had no way of knowing without testing it. We were meant to be rolling it out to just 1 percent of users, but my fictional bug threatened to push the update live for everyone.

It was enough to get me out of the pitches, and I later learned I'd picked a good time to skive. Flick said they were terrible, an utter waste of time and resources. But whatever. By the end of it, John had picked the final employees to accompany us to New York. We only had a dozen days to go until the ceremony, and the founders were already stressed out about it. And they weren't the only ones under a lot of pressure.

***

My body was worn out, and I started feeling ill. It wasn't like a normal sickness, though. Sure, I threw up all the time, hardly slept and couldn't swallow solid food, but it was more than that. It was in my head and beneath my skin, and despite the doctor's reassurances that it was stress-related and that I should try to rest and recuperate, I still worried I had cancer or some sort of internal haemorrhaging. The anxiety was the worst part, but I couldn't afford to let it affect my work. There was too much to do, and I was often the only one who actually knew how to do things.

By the time that we flew to Disrupt, my body had given up and so had I. It felt like my purpose in life was to work until I dropped, like even prison or death would be better than being in purgatory. Even the medication did little to help – a cocktail of hyoscine butylbromide and citalopram to calm my stomach and to stabilise my moods. The stress of work, combined with the long hours, gave me palpitations and a deep, dark fear of the future.

"Don't go to New York," Flick had said, cupping a cold hand around the back of my neck. "I'm serious, Dan. You're exhausted, and you need a rest. Tell John you can't go."

"Hell no," I replied. "He'll kill me!"

"Yeah? Well, if you go, you'll kill yourself, and then what am I going to do?"

Flick had got a point, but I felt like I had no choice. I felt a lot better after we landed, although I had a moment as I passed through security and started struggling to breathe. The flight attendants almost refused to let me board until John leapt to my defence.

Once we were safely on-board, he leaned in and whispered, "What the hell do you think you're doing, Dan? Are you trying to fuck this up for us?"

I had no reply, but luckily he let it lie. He was in good spirits again by the time that we landed, a state of cheerful optimism which he maintained until the following evening, the evening of the ceremony.

It was an unusual night, and one of the only times I ever saw the founders wearing suits. We'd all scrubbed up for the occasion. The guys were wearing tuxedos and shiny black shoes, and Flick, as the only woman, stood out like a thing of beauty in the middle of a warzone, a stunning creature in a soft blue dress.

I was feeling a little better – well enough to eat and drink – and the ceremony started without incident. The food was fantastic, little canapes passed around on silver platters, and rich ingredients I'd never even heard of. The champagne was flowing and I was in a jolly mood before I knew it, a mood which turned sour when the night took an unpleasant turn.

The shit went down when Former.ly was up for its first award, Best New Start-up, which John and Peter thought was already in the bag. It turned out that they were wrong. When the host called out another name, John's face turned scarlet. He just couldn't stand another company picking up the trophy and being the centre of attention, but he shouldn't have worried. Former.ly was about to get some attention of its own.

The two founders shot to their feet in disbelief, and the cameras that were panning the crowd homed in on them. It started off as a shouting match with John and Peter screaming into each other's faces, but it soon turned into a brawl. I held back, but my stomach lurched as Flick rushed forward to fill the gap between Nils, who was pulling his fist back, and the face of a scraggy-haired tech geek who happened to be in the wrong place at the wrong time.

That's where things started to get hazy. I stood up and went after Flick. A couple of seconds later, I took a knee to the head and a fist to the chin and crumbled to the floor.

***

When I came round in the back of the ambulance, I saw John sitting there beside me, one hand clutching a cold compress to a swollen eyelid while the other eye glared back at me. I could tell that he wasn't happy.

They took us to the hospital to check us over. John was released, but they kept me in for observation. My blood pressure was above normal and I had a mild concussion, but really, they were more concerned about the palpitations that I kept having.

As I lay in the hospital bed that evening, tossing and turning whilst I tried to get to sleep, I flicked arbitrarily through TV channels in search of something to fall asleep to, a talk show to keep me company or a rerun of *Top Gear* to take the edge off things. When I reached the news, my blood ran cold and I sat bolt upright in bed.

A familiar face was looking back at me through the screen. Peter was being interviewed by a reporter, and he'd spruced himself up with wax in his hair and an expensive suit that he'd bought back before Former.ly moved stateside.

"We have a unique opportunity," he was saying. "Most social networking sites are constrained by the number of people who are currently alive. We, on the other hand, will only grow and grow as time and generations go by."

"But how does that help your company?"

"Let's put it this way," Peter replied. "According to a guy called Carl Haub, who's a demographer, over a hundred billion people have died since 50,000 B.C. That might sound like a lot, but as the population increases, so does the number of people who die. All of our competitors are limited to the current population of the earth. We can tap into that and augment it with the legions of the dead. That means that our potential user-base is as close to infinite as you can get."

"But how can someone be a user if they're dead?"

Peter laughed at the question and dragged a hand through his roguish hair. "Other social networks are limited by the number of people on the planet," he said. "You can't be an active user if you're dead. We're different. Former.ly defines an active user as anyone whose profile is accessed, either from the back end of the site if they're alive or from their memorial page if they're dead. Our user base is growing exponentially. If you take the current mortality rate and factor in our growth rate and the rising population of the planet, we expect to hit fifteen billion before 2100 and fifty billion before 2200, maybe sooner."

"Big plans indeed," the anchor said. "But perhaps a little far-fetched. Social networking is still in its relative infancy, after all."

The cameras drifted and the shot shifted to an aerial view of the company's headquarters. Peter clearly had more to say, but the reporter refused to give his crazy claims the airtime that they (probably) deserved.

As for me, I didn't care. I was just glad to be away from the office. I booted up my laptop, loaded a web browser, pointed it at Former.ly and logged into my profile for the first time in months.

※

The hospital released me the following day with a possible diagnosis – anxiety disorder brought on by the stress of working at Former.ly. They suggested arranging a consultation with a local doctor and suggested some therapy techniques in the meantime. Then they checked me out and unleashed me on the world again. I caught a flight back to California a couple of days later.

John and Peter didn't seem pleased to see me when I pulled up outside the complex, but then I was happy with anything short of open hostility. In their eyes and in the eyes of the rest of the team, I'd deserted the company in its hour of need. "Sorry" just wasn't going to cut it, but that didn't stop me from saying it.

"Save your apologies," John replied. "You might need 'em later. Right now, we need you at your desk."

"Why?" I asked. "What's new?"

"We're working on a new feature, and we're going to need your help on it. It's a biggie, and according to our prelim tests, it'll help to increase revenue and engagement simultaneously. We did some work on it while you were away, but we need a little magic to speed it up ahead of the beta launch."

"What kind of feature are we talking about?" I asked.

"It's pretty simple, really," John replied. "We want to add a ticker on the back end of the site so that when you're viewing your dashboard, you can see who died and when, with a particular focus on friends and family."

"Why?" I asked again. "What's the point?"

"The point?" John laughed. "If we remind people that their friends are dead, they're more likely to stay on the site for long enough to post a message of remembrance. Time is money and money is money, and the more we can milk from our users, the better."

When he put it like that, he had a point. In fact, it was so simple that I was surprised we hadn't thought of it before. John quickly gave me some instructions. When I was happy with what he wanted me to do, I wandered over to my desk, booted up my computer and got to work.

CHAPTER EIGHTEEN

IT WAS A BUSY WEEK, but I somehow knew it was for the best. I kept myself so busy that I hardly noticed how ill I felt, although when I went to the bathroom it was a different story altogether, as though all of the stress was coming to the surface. I tried not to breathe too much because the doctor had said that breathing too much could only make things worse. If you breathe too much, you hyperventilate, and if you hyperventilate, you start to panic.

As if my body didn't hate me enough, the sheer brutality of the working hours after the sudden peace and quiet led me to develop a typist's hunch, the pain you feel when you've been bending over a machine for too long. My salary just about stretched to a couple of sessions with a chiropractor, but even with a strong set of painkillers and a purpose-built workstation with a high monitor and an ergonomic chair, the long hours in the office took their toll.

To make matters worse, my bed broke. It was one of those crappy flat packs, designed for sleeping and nothing else. A couple of the wooden slats snapped in half, and it started a downward spiral that left me wondering whether lying on the floor would be more comfortable.

"It's murder on my back," I complained when Flick and I were hanging out after a particularly stressful day. "But I can't afford to buy a new one."

"What about John and Peter?" she said.

"What about them?" I laughed. "I asked for a

replacement, and they refused."

The following night, when everyone was asleep, I broke the frame apart and stashed it in the bins outside, then laid the mattress on the floor and climbed beneath the duvet. I didn't know it at the time, but I'd sleep like that for the rest of my stay in Palo Alto.

***

The mood was subdued at the breakfast table and the gloom seemed to be spreading. Kerry hardly touched his cooked breakfast, and he usually ate as though he was expecting to never eat again. Flick nursed a cup of coffee in silence, eventually downing it when it was cold. Then, Kerry broke the tension with a nervous cough.

"Guys," he said. "I have something to tell you, and I wanted you to know now before I go and tell the bosses. I'm leaving Former.ly."

Flick gasped, and I almost choked on my cereal. Kerry was one of the first four to join the company, and I couldn't imagine working without him. It didn't help that he was physically huge and that he never seemed to leave the office, meaning he was always around if you needed him. Sure, we usually didn't need him, but that wasn't the point.

"I'm happy for you," I said, cautiously. "And I'm sure John and Peter will be too."

"Oh hell no," he groaned, throwing a paper serviette on to his plate and covering his face with his hands. "That's not true, and you know it as well as I do. They'll kill me!"

"Don't be stupid, Kerry," Flick said, scooting over and trying to put an arm around him. She had to settle for stretching it two thirds of the way around his vast, heaving back. I'd seen Kerry face off against six-foot skinheads in bars, but John and Peter had got him as scared and repentant as a dog that's torn apart a living room. "You'll be fine. We'll make sure of it. Right, guys?"

Nobody moved. We had a sixth sense for trouble, and it seemed prudent to stay schtum, especially because John and Peter had sidled over to the table. John started to clap, slowly. The sound echoed eerily around the quiet kitchen.

***

"Fantastic performance," John said, breaking the silence with a sense of lingering finality. "And when exactly were you going to come and talk to us, Kerry?"

The videographer said nothing. He just sat there, clearly shaken and unable to continue eating. Flick pouted and tried to leap to his defence, but the founders were having none of it.

"Know your place, woman," John snarled. "And see that you stick to it. The same goes for you too, Dan. Get back to your breakfast, or fuck off back to work if you've finished. We've got a business to run."

I got up first, and Flick and Kerry soon followed. When Peter saw him standing, however, he decided it was time to say something. "Kerry," he said. "Sit back down. We need to talk to you."

I shot Flick a worried glance as I was leaving, but she just shrugged her shoulders and wandered off to put some music on the jukebox. With nothing else to do, I went to sit down at my desk, but I couldn't get any work done. No one could. We were dying to know what was happening.

At last, after a tense half hour, something happened. Kerry came strolling purposefully through the office with no emotion on his pallid face. He said nothing, which was unusual enough, walked over to his desk and started packing his possessions into a rucksack.

"I'll send a van to get the rest of my stuff," he announced. "It's been fun, guys. Good luck with Former.ly. You're going to need it."

***

That week seemed to drag on and to rush by simultaneously. The loss of Kerry left a gap in the atmosphere, and it was taking some serious getting used to. As for Flick, my relationship with her was strained at best.

When bad luck strikes, it seldom strikes once, and when it came to Former.ly, bad luck was like a plague from a vengeful god. Flick took the call with the bad news, then took me aside and passed it on to me. I took a couple of moments to compose myself, and then I used my limited authority to call an immediate all-hands team meeting.

"Glad you could all make it," I began. The room could barely contain all of the faces, most of which were relatively new to me. I realised that, despite a couple of high-profile departures, the company was still growing at an alarming rate.

"Now, I don't mean to cause a panic," I began. "But we have a situation, one which threatens the entire company with a wave of controversy. I hope you folks can handle it."

"Get to the point, Dan."

"Okay, okay," I said. "Here's the deal. Kerry's mom just called. She asked me to pass a message on. Kerry had a heart attack."

***

Kerry's condition was stable, and John stopped me from rushing straight over like I wanted to. He let Flick leave early though, and she kept me up-to-date throughout the

afternoon. By knocking off time at six PM, Kerry's condition
was improving. When I actually finished work at seven
thirty, I booked a taxi and promised the driver an extra ten
bucks if he got me to the hospital by eight.

He pulled up in an ambulance bay at seven fifty-five,
and I gave him his bonus as promised, before legging it
through the hospital at random. It was a doomed mission, as
I'd always known it would be. They weren't letting anyone
in after eight, and it was quarter past by the time that I
found the ward.

Flick called me over as I walked past the waiting room.
She was the only one left in there, biting her fingernails to
the quick as she stared at the doorway, at the face of every
stranger who walked past until I came into view.

"It's too late," she said, hugging me frostily and
gesturing for me to sit down. I ignored her and stayed on my
feet. "I held them off for as long as I could, but they said
you'll have to come back in the morning. He needs his sleep.
He keeps drifting in and out of consciousness."

"I want to see him," I insisted, stubbornly. I tried talking
to one of the nurses, pleading my case and even pretending
to be his brother. It didn't work, but they did take down my
details and promise to call me if his condition changed.

Kerry's heart attack had hit me hard; it brought back
memories of Abhi's death and his subsequent send-off in
North London. It was all too much for me, and I collapsed
onto Flick's shoulder, chest heaving with tears that wouldn't
come out.

***

Sleep didn't come to me that evening, and the following
day was a blur of bleak despair. I still couldn't get anything,
but John wouldn't let me take the day off and so I did my

best to crack on with the code that I was meant to be working on.

Bad news struck again that evening; the darkest news always seems to come at night. The hospital called, while I was dozing in and out of consciousness with a crap comedy on my laptop. They had an update about Kerry's condition. It wasn't good.

I cried. Then I found Flick and told her what she'd been hoping no one would ever tell her. Misery loves company, and all that we had was each other. I started sobbing again, and the two of us cried ourselves to sleep in each other's arms.

CHAPTER NINETEEN

MORALE WAS LOW. Morale was very low. I broke the bad news to the rest of the team the following morning, after they climbed one by one out of their beds and walked into the kitchen for breakfast. Once I told the first couple of people, I didn't have to do much more. Bad news spread quickly at Former.ly.

And so the mood was subdued over the next couple of days. Even the newer folks, who hadn't known Kerry for as long as I had, seemed shaken by his loss. We all talked in hushed whispers, and tears were pretty common when people thought that no one else was looking. Kerry was a figurehead, a real character. I'll never meet anyone else quite like him.

Out of respect for our old friend, we got our heads down and poured everything we had into the company. Whether Kerry would've approved or not was immaterial because the company was the only thing that linked us all together.

On a mild, dry Tuesday, the week after Kerry's death and two days before the memorial service, we opened the doors of the office to an unwelcome visitor, a familiar face from across the pond. I knew him as Sam Whitehouse, the cop who kept showing up at the old office.

"Hi, chaps," he said, sauntering into the office like he owned the place. Nils was standing reluctantly beside him; John growled out a simple order: "Don't let him out of your sight."

"Mr. Policeman," Peter replied, light-heartedly. "So nice of you to join us, and from such a long way away too. To what do we owe the pleasure?"

"Oh nothing, nothing at all. No, no, I'm over here on holiday, so I thought I'd swing by to say hello. It's a beautiful part of the world."

"Yes, it is," replied Peter. "That's why we decided to move over here. How long are you staying for, Inspector…?"

"You can call me Sam," he said. "I don't think I've had the pleasure of meeting you, Mr. Bow, although I know who you are. I'll be over here for a week. A policeman's wages don't stretch as far as they used to, and I've got to fund the wife and kids too. But a week should be more than enough to find out what's going on around here, I'm sure."

"And what exactly do you think is going on, Sam?" Peter said. "Innocent until proven guilty, right? You've levelled some pretty serious accusations in the past. And besides, isn't this out of your jurisdiction?"

"Of course, it's out of my jurisdiction," he laughed. "I'm not looking for anything, if that's what you mean. I thought I'd stop by and see what you boys have been up to. What with you being famous and all."

"Well," John said, taking him by the arm and beginning to show him around the office. "You're more than welcome to stop by any time. Come on, let me give you the tour."

***

Money had always been tight, but nobody realised quite how bad our finances actually were. We'd started to receive final demands for our utilities, and the company cupboards grew bare. It had nothing to do with our investors – the money was still there, but it was locked up in assets and cash flow was becoming a problem.

Shortly after Sam's visit, the first people started to leave. The closest the founders came to publicly acknowledging the departures was when they evasively explained that certain job roles were being outsourced to Eastern Europe where it was cheaper. When I realised how bad our finances were, I started to wonder whether the company could survive at all.

Meanwhile, we'd been offered help from an unexpected source. The story, as Peter explained it, was this. One day, while he was talking to John about the staff and promising to raise more money from the investors, they were interrupted by a knock at the door. The two founders looked at each other, and John shouted "come in" over his shoulder.

Nate, the company's cleaner, wandered in, sheepishly dragging a Hoover behind him. We used to joke that we always saw him carrying it and never saw him using it, but he kept the place clean enough, even if he did seem to pop up at unusual hours. We were an unusual company. As long as he didn't turn the Hoover on in the middle of the night, he was fine by us. And now he was standing in front of the two founders and leaning on it like a crutch.

"I won't beat around the bush," he said. "I've heard what people are saying. You guys are out of money."

Peter opened his mouth to argue, but John beat him to it. "What's it to you?" he asked.

"Oh, nothing," Nate replied. "It's just that I'm a programmer myself. You know, before I ended up working here, I had my own business. I made some bad decisions, I guess. I mean, we all do at some point. Anyway, I'm here now and I'm willing to work for you, in exchange for shares in the company. Nothing major, just enough to make it worth my while when you guys go public. So what do you say? Do I get the job?"

Peter smiled and winked at John. "Bring in a résumé and a code sample on Monday," he said. "We'll give you a trial run and talk about compensation if you pass the first two weeks. Oh, and you'll still need to carry out your cleaning duties. It's starting to look like a shit-heap around here."

And so, just like that, and once again without comment from senior management, we were joined by a new programmer. One who I'd have to work closely with if we ever wanted to ship some of the features I was working on.

CHAPTER TWENTY

PETER STARTED SMOKING WEED AGAIN. You could see it in his eyes, which were redder than hell. He used to show up for breakfast stinking of grass. Occasionally, late at night or during one of our arbitrary parties, he would pass a joint around and talk about the good old days. Mostly, I figured it was just for show.

I was starting to feel good about life again. Then, I remembered that Abhi and Kerry were dead and that there was no such thing as normal at Former.ly, as Nils and his team proved when we had an unexpected visitor on a Thursday evening. The first thing I knew about it was a sound like a fox with its tail caught in a door, a deathly howl which seemed to claw at the soul. I ran outside to investigate and saw Nils and his men swarming around a guy with a balaclava over his face, who was trying to protect himself against the onslaught of their fists and heavy truncheons.

I struggled with my conscience for a second, and my conscience lost. I secreted myself in the shadows, pulled the hood of my jumper over my eyes, and waited, watching. When I thought that the intruder could take no more, that his skull would be pounded into the dust outside the office, Nils gave the order to stop and they backed away slightly as the masked figure retched and choked in the gravel.

"Take off his mask," Nils growled. Two men stepped forward and removed the balaclava, while he shone his torch in the intruder's face. From my vantage point, I could just make out a flash of white flesh and a pair of terrified eyes, but I wouldn't have moved closer if you'd paid me. "Who are you?"

There was no response; Nils pulled back his arm and delivered a sharp backhand, which cracked the visitor across the face and sent him reeling to the floor, and then he asked the question again. "Who are you?" There was no reply, except for a stifled sob from the injured man.

"Right," Nils said, turning his back on his victim to face his men. "Cuff him and get him out of here before someone shows up. See what you can find out about who he is and who sent him. Do what you've got to do and then take him for a little drive. Go, now."

His henchmen were quick to oblige. They handcuffed their prisoner and slipped a hood over his head, then guided him into the back of one of their black SUVs and skidded away from the compound. Only Nils remained, staring thoughtfully out into the night. After a minute or two, he lit a cigarette, and I backed slowly away and returned sheepishly to my room. I'd already been on his bad side once. I had no desire to make things worse.

***

On Saturday, we hit a new milestone. User sign-ups hit their highest ever rate, with half a million new users joining Former.ly every day. It was beyond our wildest dreams. While the site wasn't exactly making money, it was at least paying the bills. We weren't bothered; rumours of an IPO were afoot. If we could last until then, we'd be able to cash in our shares and become rich overnight.

As a consequence, we threw a party, and it was one hell of a night. It was like the good old days, and even though Nils and his men were still on duty, they got involved with a couple of the drinking games. Flick looked stunning in a tight black dress, but she was exhausted from pulling all-nighters and she passed out by midnight. I tucked her into her bed, locked the door and then left her to it.

The party started to wind down just after four o'clock in the morning. I was in the car park, sharing a joint with Peter, when he said something that surprised me. We were both drunk, but we'd both been drunker. I'd hit the barrier and come out the other side, and even though I'd carried on drinking, I couldn't get any drunker. It just made my heart race.

"Dan," he began, pausing to take another suck at the roach before flicking the ash and passing it over to me. "Listen. John and I have been talking, and I want to make a proposition. We want you to come on-board as a minority partner. We need someone we can trust, and you're the only one."

"What about Flick?" I asked.

"It's true that she's been here longer, but longevity doesn't equal trust. Besides, she had a hiatus. No, it has to be you, Dan."

"What exactly are you asking me to do?" I said.

"You'll join the board and have a say in the way that the business evolves. You'll look after the place when the two of us aren't around. You'll get cash, a bonus and shares. The longer you stay with us, the more you earn our trust and the more responsibility you'll have."

I handed the joint back to him, sat for a second and made my decision. "I'm in," I said. "I've got no idea why, but I'm in."

CHAPTER TWENTY-ONE

TWO DAYS LATER, Flick and I were alone in my bedroom. She was sitting on the room's only chair as we streamed Netflix from my machine. She'd been quiet all evening, barely breathing a word, but suddenly she spoke.

"God, I'd love to take this company down," she said.

"And I'd love to help you," I replied. "But what's it to you?"

"Don't bullshit me, Dan. We both know that John and Peter are up to something. They killed Abhi. I know it. They probably killed Kerry too. We need to do something."

I sighed. "It's funny you should mention it," I said. "I have a plan. But I'll need your help."

"Dan, I'd like nothing better than to help you. What's the plan?"

I paused for a moment, deep in thought, before I answered. "I'm not quite sure," I said. "But I think it'll develop over time. You're in the perfect place to help me out here, and I already have my diaries and the code that I've written. But it's not just that. There's something else going on here. I don't know what it is, but I intend to find out. And I want you to help me."

"Sure, I'll do anything."

"Peter's taken me into his confidence," I explained. "And it looks like I'm about to get closer to the founders than ever before. Perhaps that'll help. Maybe I'll learn something we can use. I want you to keep your eyes and ears open. You know everything that goes on around here, so tell me everything you know. In particular, keep your eyes on the founders, and keep a log of where they go and who they speak to. But keep it analogue, and don't let anyone else know about it. I don't even want you to tell me where it is. You understand?"

"Gotcha," she said.

"I mean it, Flick. We've got to be careful, careful like you wouldn't believe. Trust no one, and don't computerise anything unless you have to. Who knows what tech they've got in place to track our movements? I wouldn't be surprised if the rooms are bugged. In future, we'd better meet elsewhere."

"Jesus, Dan, since when have you been so paranoid?"

"Since I realised that everyone else in this building is out to get me," I said.

**

In the end, to avoid suspicion, I alternated between writing in my journal, which was hidden in a secret place off-campus, and updating my profile on Former.ly. I had no way of proving it, of course, but it made sense to assume that the two founders had the ability to access the site's database, to de-encrypt the data and to read it at their leisure. With Former.ly's founders, I always assumed the worst, and the fact that it was theoretically possible was enough to scare me into filling my profile with false information, just in case.

But it was in my journal that I was totally honest, particularly now that I had a plan. If Flick and I were going to take down the founders, we'd need as much information as possible, and words really can be weapons. My journal was an important part of the plan, and so as much as it was a ball-ache to write by hand when I can type one hundred and thirty words per minute, it was also a necessity.

The sad thing was, I loved Former.ly. It was like a child to me, and I was beginning to suspect that the site housed more of my code than anyone else's, even though John and Peter bootstrapped the damn thing from a bedroom. But times had changed, and new features demanded significant rewrites and whole swathes of new code. We'd also been forced to upgrade to a new database to keep the site secure and to make sure that it wouldn't collapse under its own weight.

Of course, when all the variables changed and we needed someone to manually make all of the changes in the code, the job fell to the monkeys at the bottom of the ladder. We'd stopped taking on interns, but we did hire coders from Stanford University, who were graduating and who wanted to stay in the area at all costs, even if it meant taking the lowest salary that John and Peter could get away with paying them.

That was what was going through my mind as I wrote in my journal – not Flick's lips, but the faces of the people that the company had crushed along the way. I counted myself as one of them, although I wasn't sure why. I stood to make some serious money if the company went public, enough to retire on. So why did I want it to fail?

***

Operation Nemesis, as Flick and I were calling it, was a slow burner. To protect ourselves if we ever got caught, we made sure that neither of us knew what the other was doing.

I was given a little extra ammunition one evening when the office was virtually deserted. Flick was waiting for me to finish coding so we could kick back and watch Netflix, probably passed out on my bed. I, meanwhile, was trying my best to gather intel by working overtime. The only problem was that everyone else had given up and gone to bed, and I was still sat there trying to iron out a couple more bugs.

I made it until one o'clock in the morning, and then I got up from my desk to make another cup of coffee. The source code was beginning to warp and meld in front of my eyes, dancing across the screen. And I still had a couple of hours to go.

The place was deserted when I snuck into the kitchen, but by the time I found some milk, there was the distant murmur of conversation in the air. I followed the sound towards the boardroom and then melted into the shadows as I got closer to the door and saw what was happening. I wasn't the only one with an interest in the conversation.

It was Nate, the cleaner. He was trying to look as though he was cleaning the skirting board, but the sponge in his hand was bone dry and I watched him for a good thirty seconds. He wasn't cleaning shit. He was eavesdropping, and that meant I couldn't get any closer without being seen. I'd just decided to confront him when the door opened and the two founders stepped out. They didn't even look at Nate, who was back to cleaning the skirting boards with his dry sponge, and I had to back even further into the shadows to stop them from seeing me. It was a close call.

As soon as I knew that the coast was clear, I stepped out into the hallway, just in time to grab Nate by the collar as he tried to beat a hasty retreat. He was the smaller man, and my momentum took the two of us crashing into the wall. His sunken eyes admitted defeat the second they clocked on to me, but that didn't stop him from trying to wriggle away.

"What the hell do you want?" he panted.

His pupils dilated as I tightened my grip and watched

him squirm. He knew he was in trouble. There was an extra irony in the fact that if I attacked him, he'd have to call for the security team, who would hit him too if they found out what he was up to. I let him plead with me, though his words fell on deaf ears. When he repeated his question, I answered him in a word, "Information."

"I don't understand," he replied.

"Then let me explain. It's simple, really. I want to know what you heard. Not just that, though – more. Everything else you've overheard, and everything you hear in the future."

"Yeah?" Nate laughed. "What's in it for me?"

"Well," I said. "For a start, you might get to keep your teeth. And your job, for that matter. Besides, I can pay you, if you find out what I need to know."

"How much?" he asked.

"I'll decide that based on what you tell me," I replied. "And I'll need proof too. The more comprehensive the proof is, the greater your reward."

He was silent for a couple of seconds whilst he thought about it. Then, he realised he was out of options, and I watched as his eyes glazed over.

"Okay," he said. "I'm in. Now let me down." I loosened my grip – not too much, just enough to make sure that he could breathe. "What's it to you, anyway? And how do I know you're going to come up with the goods if I help you?"

"The first question is none of your business," I replied. "And as for the second, you're going to have to trust me. And you'd better trust me quickly because I'm about the only friend you've got around here."

"You're not my friend," he scowled.

"No," I replied. "I'm not. But I'm about to be. Better get ready to trust me, Nate, 'cause you're going to tell me everything you know."

CHAPTER TWENTY-TWO

NATE OBEYED HIS ORDERS, and I started to receive a steady trickle of information, which I recorded in my journal. Apparently, John and Peter had been talking about China and Peter's sketchy acquaintances over there. According to Nate, John wasn't happy with the way things were going, but Peter stood his ground. No resolution was reached, and that's when the conversation abruptly ended and they came walking out the door.

At least, that's what Nate told me. Since I had no reason to doubt him, it's what I had to go with. I hadn't learned anything new since then, but that was about to change. He'd sent me a text to say he had some news and arranged to meet me at a coffee shop. I didn't have long to wait.

"Let's get down to business," Nate said, as he slid into the seat beside me. "I just want to get this over and done with."

"Sure thing," I replied. "Now tell me why you brought me here. What do I need to know?"

"The president has joined Former.ly," he said, his eyes darting to the doors and back. "I got an e-mail that John sent to Peter. He said he wanted to step up security and to have a dedicated server for his profile."

"That's pretty big news. Can you get me a copy of the e-mail?"

"Way ahead of you," he said, passing me a crumpled printout from a plastic folder. "I'm checking all of the bins, but you know what they're like. They're not the type to leave a paper trail. John shreds everything, and I don't think Peter even knows how to use the printer. But they're not immune to everything. I have my ways. Keyloggers, backdoors, and that sort of thing."

"How does that work?" I asked.

"Basically, it registers every keystroke and every click, then transmits it wirelessly to a receiver. Then, I just filter through the data and reconstruct whatever it was that they were doing."

"I see," I said. "Just get me what you can get me, Nate. I'll do the rest."

He left shortly afterwards, and we both made our separate ways back to the office.

**

A couple of days later, Former.ly held a press conference, which was live-streamed across the internet. John started the announcement with his co-founder to his left and an American flag billowing in an artificial wind behind them. They were broadcasting from the boardroom, but we weren't allowed inside, so we had to watch it around the kitchen table on a MacBook.

"Ladies and gentlemen of the world," John began, staring straight into the barrel of the camera and right back out at the viewer. "Thank you for joining us today, on what is a historic day for Former.ly and for the world." John paused slightly for effect and then continued.

"Former.ly has been through a lot to get here, and we're committed to staying at the top of our game. We know that the wisdom of the masses often outweighs the wisdom of the few. We're also hiring, and we need the brightest minds of our generation. So we've devised a little game for you.

Peter?" He gestured for his co-founder to take the lead and stepped backwards slightly to avoid the limelight.

"Thanks, John," he said. "Much appreciated. Now, as you guys know, we take data protection seriously. If our users don't trust us to look after their data then they won't use our service. It's as simple as that. We already know that we have some of the best security on the market, and we're pretty confident in our ability to repel attackers. However, it could always be even better."

Peter paused to take a sip from his glass of water before continuing. The other two men stayed stationary, and the flag continued to billow in the breeze. Beside me, one of our junior programmers stifled a cough.

"So here's the deal," Peter continued. "We want you guys to try to hack us. You name it, we think we're ready for it. Whether we're talking about DDoS attacks, security flaws or database compromises, we want you to find out about it."

"And why are we doing this, Peter?" John asked, leaning forward slightly.

"Well, John, I'm glad you asked. We're augmenting our developer team, and I think that you'll find we can offer something that most of our competitors can't – excitement. Let's face it, everyone and their dog wants to work for us because everyone and their dog is talking about us. Former.ly's the coolest kid at school."

"So how do people get the jobs, Pete?" Perhaps it seemed natural to the thousands of outsiders who were watching, but I knew that this was just the latest act in the John and Peter show. They'd rehearsed this, for sure.

"It's easy enough," he replied. "If you want a job, you've got to earn it. We want you to do what you can to try to break our site, and then we want you to help us to fix it. We take our users' security seriously here at Former.ly. If there are any vulnerabilities, we want to know about them before anyone else does. Oh, and guess what. We'll hand-pick the best bug finders to come and join us here in Palo Alto. We're going to change the world together, folks. You heard it here first."

***

The response from the public was phenomenal, and we quickly took on a dozen of the best bug finders to help us to deal with the fallout. Our servers were taking a pummelling – a heavier pummelling than we'd been expecting – but we were still agile enough to avoid going under. One of the bugs was so serious that an attacker gained admin access to the database, and another could've compromised unencrypted login details for all of our users in Germany. Luckily, we were able to get the bugs fixed with no long-term damage.

We still didn't have enough programmers, but we were struggling to find the right talent in the States. Luckily, Peter had his eyes on China again, and he was working on setting up a second office in the Middle Kingdom.

"China is calling," Peter explained, as he announced the news to a packed crowd of employees. By now, we were meeting in the garden because it was the only way to fit everyone in the same place. It was nice to sit outside in the Cali sunshine, even in the winter, but there was a darker side to it. Nils and his armed henchmen were never far away, a harsh reminder that the two founders didn't trust us.

"Over half of our bug finders are from China," John explained. "And it's also our fastest-growing market. We're one of the few Western companies to have cracked it. Setting up shop in Beijing makes perfect political and practical sense. Think about it. We can provide a better service for our users, and we can recruit some local talent at the same time."

"Precisely," said Peter. "And it'll help me to score some brownie points with my contacts too. It's a no-brainer. We've talked it through and there's literally no way that this could backfire on us. Even money's not an object. If we burn our fingers, we burn our fingers, close the office and swallow the loss. Ladies and gentlemen, Former.ly is taking over China."

CHAPTER TWENTY-THREE

THE CHINESE INVASION took place with all of the speed and efficiency of a bulldozer building a house. We made slow progress and got used to seeing lawyers around the office. When the first guy came in, we all knew what he was. Sometimes you can tell that a guy is a lawyer just by looking at him, like you can spot a programmer by his ponytail and his Dungeons & Dragons T-shirt.

There was an army of lawyers, invading the compound one soldier at a time. When I plucked up the courage to ask Peter what the hell was going on, he was evasive.

"All I can tell you, Dan," he said, "is that Chinese law has a lot of nuances. We don't want to get shut down before we've even started."

"Where did we get the money to pay for them?" I asked, but Peter just tapped the side of his nose and told me to keep quiet.

The lawyers weren't our only unexpected visitors. Less than a week after the founders' announcement, Elaine flew over from London. She was working full-time now and heading up a small army of accountants who were still back in the UK. Nate said she wasn't happy. She was doing the work of a finance director, but without the status, the title or the salary.

She arrived around lunchtime, walking into the office unannounced and handing out free hugs to anyone who wanted one, including the folks she'd never met. There were more new faces than old ones, but she still swept down on everyone in sight like a drunk mother at her daughter's birthday party.

"Elaine!" I beamed when my turn came round. "Long time no see! What's new?"

"It's a long story," she replied. There was something furtive about her expression, something that I'd never seen before. She was hiding something, presumably on the founders' orders. "Times are busy, and Peter wants to keep an eye on me. You know what he's like, and now that we're setting up shop in China, there's a lot of paperwork to worry about."

"Fair enough," I said. "So how long are you staying? They haven't flown you out just for the day, have they?"

"I have no idea," Elaine replied. "I was told to pack a suitcase, to print off my ticket and to come here as quickly as possible."

"So where's your case? Let me take it in for you."

"It's back in the limo, Dan. Don't worry, I'm not staying here. It's too much for me. The boys are putting me up in a hotel."

***

I found out what was happening a couple of days later. I'd given Nate specific instructions to find out why Elaine was over here, and he didn't let me down. He arranged to meet me at the same place as before. This time, he was there first, and he'd already ordered coffees for both of us. He didn't bother to say hello.

"Got my money?" he asked. I nodded and handed over a small, bulging envelope. I'd had to dip into my savings to pay for it, but I was hoping that the information would be worth it.

"It's all in there," I said. "Now you live up to your end of the deal."

"Hey," Nate said. "Not so fast. It's not quite that simple. This wasn't a case of just finding some printouts. I had to put in a lot of work."

"Oh yeah?" I snorted. "Like what?"

"I tracked Elaine back to the hotel," he explained. "It wasn't too difficult. I found out her room number without a problem. That was the easy part. The hard part was getting her room key. I had to pay someone off."

"Excellent," I replied. "What did you find out?"

"Well, that's just the thing. I didn't find much to begin with. Just clothes and a passport. She didn't even have a laptop. I looked everywhere."

Nate paused his story to flag down a waitress for another coffee. To my mounting frustration, he waited for his drink to arrive before continuing.

"Now, where was I?" he asked. "Ah, yes. So like I said, I didn't find anything worthwhile. But I didn't stop there. I set up a couple of hidden microphones in her hotel room, just in case. I figured we might pick something up, and, with a bit of luck, they might even go unnoticed. After all, I can go back in and take them out at any time, and Nils and his men have no power outside the compound."

"Leave them there for now," I said. "What have you got for me so far?"

"I caught Elaine's end of a phone call. It sounds like big news, if you ask me. There's a lot to take in, and you're going to want to hear it yourself. Luckily for you, I made a copy."

He slid a memory stick across the table. "Take that home and listen to it," he said. "You won't be disappointed."

***

I hopped in my Tesla and drove at random until I found a quiet place to pull over. I needed privacy to listen to the recording, which I quickly did. Taking no chances, I wore headphones in case someone had bugged the car. You can never be too careful.

The recording was tinny but clearly audible, and it was clearly Elaine who was audible. I believed in its authenticity. It didn't sound edited, as though different recordings had been stitched together. It seemed to be the real deal.

You could only hear Elaine's side of the conversation, but that was all you needed. They were talking laws and protocols, looking for tax breaks and figuring out how to do something big. Something massive. Something that would change the company forever. And after listening to the recording, I knew exactly what it was.

You could tell what was happening from the questions, and while I couldn't tell who she was talking to – a stock market specialist, a fellow accountant or even the founders themselves – it was obvious what they were talking about. Former.ly was heading to the New York Stock Exchange; the company was going public.

***

Several days later, the two directors ushered me into a private room and stationed Nils outside the door with a double-barrelled shotgun in his hands.

"Sit down, Dan," John said, gesturing for me to do so. I did as I was told.

"How can I help?" I asked. Secretly, I thought I was about to get fired or worse. It was hard to tell with the founders. Right now, they were doing their best to smile, but it wasn't reassuring; it was like being winked at by a lion.

"John and I have a proposition for you," Peter said. His

face remained inscrutable. "How long have you been working at Former.ly, Dan?"

"I have no idea," I replied. Seasons seemed to come and go arbitrarily, and the move to Palo Alto had confused me. "If I had to guess," I said, "about eighteen months. Maybe two years."

"Two years sounds right to me," John said. "Truth is, we don't remember either, and neither of us can be bothered to check the records. But what we do know is that you're the most senior member of the team, both in terms of your authority over the team and in terms of the length of time you've been here."

"If you don't count Flick," I replied.

Peter flashed a half-smile at me. "Flick's not a programmer," he said. "She's a bright girl, but she doesn't know the site quite like you do. You've got a bright future ahead of you," he said. "Let's face it, Dan. We can't steer this ship alone anymore, and it'll be a cold day in hell before we bring someone in from the outside, whatever the investors say. I won't stand for it."

"And neither will I," said John. "Which is precisely why we're talking to you, Dan. We need you to take on a little extra responsibility. Think you're ready for it?"

CHAPTER TWENTY-FOUR

AS IF LIFE wasn't stressful enough already, I soon found out that my new role was more complicated than I'd been expecting. Former.ly was beginning to receive data requests from government authorities all over the world. We were talking a couple of hundred a day.

"How do you want me to deal with them?" I asked, when John and Peter first told me what was happening.

"You need to stop thinking like a developer, Dan," Peter said, gulping down a lukewarm cup of coffee. "Start thinking like a politician. That's all this game is: politics."

"Peter's right," John added. "Think of it as protecting our business interests. What will we get in return? We give nothing away for free, unless their local law forces us to."

"What do I know about local law?" I laughed. "I don't even understand the law in the U.S.!"

"You won't need to know anything," John said. "You're going to route everything through us for final sign-off anyway. There are things you don't need to know about. Deals we've made with certain authorities to share data to gain allies for Former.ly."

"I hear you," I said. It was true. I could hear him. I just couldn't understand what they were talking about.

"There are a few more things that we need to mention," John continued. "I'm going to give you a list of code names. I want you to commit those names to memory. If a request comes in using any of those code names, you approve it with no questions asked. Memorise them after this conversation, and then burn the paper so that no one else can find it."

"There are two key things to remember," John continued. "First, if the request is made by the American government or by any person of authority within it, you are to proceed no further and to forward the case to me. Do you understand me, Dan? We're talking about national security. I'm not fucking around here."

"Yeah," I said. "I hear you. What's the other thing?"

"Same deal," said Peter, simply. "But with our Asian friends. If the request comes from China, you're to stop what you're doing and to forward it to me. Are we clear?"

"We're clear," I said, though I felt anything but. I had a suspicion to confirm, but I couldn't just flat out ask them. I'd have to get Nate to look into it.

I suspected that the founders were playing the two great governments against each other. If they were, it was a dangerous game to play.

***

I learned even more about my role in the coming weeks, and I didn't pretend that I liked what I learned. But I didn't have much of a choice, and so I went along with it in spite of my better judgement. By that point, I was in over my head, and I had nothing left to lose.

I had a further shock one evening when John, Peter and I were working late in the boardroom while everyone else was in bed. They liked me to make my reports at random times in the dead of night, so that no one could overhear us. We'd been talking about those damned data requests again. I hated those things.

"I just don't get it," I said. "Why hand over data at all?"

John shook his head. "That's not how it works, Dan.

Trust me. We've put a lot of thought into this. This is way above your paygrade."

"But perhaps if we could just…"

"No!" John exclaimed. "Listen to me. There's a reason why we operate the way we operate. You're not in possession of all the facts."

"And what are the facts?" I asked. "Face it, guys. You never share anything. How am I supposed to help if you don't trust me?"

John paused for a moment, deep in thought. He looked at Peter, and Peter stared straight back at him. John blinked and turned away, and Peter said, "Tell him." John sighed.

"Very well," he replied, morosely. "But it's against my better judgement. I'm blaming you if this comes back to bite us in the ass."

"You blame me for everything anyway," Peter laughed.

"It's because it's always your fucking fault," John snapped. "Just like this will be your fault."

"I can keep a secret," I replied.

"Yeah, you'd better," he said. "What I'm about to tell you can never leave this room. We can't cut off the data supply to the government because the government is where we get our data from. Specifically, the British, Chinese and American governments. If they don't have the data themselves, they can get hold of it."

"What data?" I asked. "What could be so important that we'd we leak confidential information to get it?"

"You just don't get it, do you? That's how we know when our users die, although you wouldn't know it. Notifications from family members can only get us so far, and they're often incorrectly filed."

John paused for a second to catch his breath before dropping his bombshell. "Eighty-five percent of our profiles are online because of our agreements with various governments. They feed us their death records in real-time. In return, we grant them access to our database. They like to check up on criminals and perverts, that sort of thing. They want to see what they're up to before the bad guys are too dead to face justice. Without those records, we're nothing."

**

The full enormity of what I'd learned took a little while to sink in, but it was driven home every time I had to process one of the data requests. Still, it made decisions easier, so I got to spend more time coding.

We were working on the user interface, something that Flick was trying to win awards for – we were basing the changes on the latest batch of results from our user surveys, and combining that with real-time data on how people were using the site. It was pretty cool stuff, but it was difficult.

We had other problems too. Employees were leaving the company in droves, but never with concrete reasons. They talked about how the company was doomed, how they could no longer support its ethos, and how better opportunities had come along, but we all knew it for what it was – a morale problem. As for the founders, they just didn't care. After all, why should they? For every disgruntled American employee, there were a dozen in China who'd take half the salary.

**

The trouble all started when the police showed up, again. This time, they weren't from Scotland Yard. They were from the Palo Alto Police Department, and they weren't here to talk about Abhi. The cops back home had filed his death as unsolved and moved on. It was nothing personal. The money just wasn't there. Under a conservative government and as the son of two foreign nationals, he had no chance.

But Kerry was an American citizen, born and bred in the land of the free. He was also male, white, and reasonably rich, and the third unexpected death to hit the company, so the police took his death more seriously. As far as the initial investigation went, it was an open and shut case. He'd had a heart attack, which isn't unusual for a man of his size and disposition, and then he'd had another one at the hospital.

I was about to find out that perhaps it wasn't as simple as that after all.

***

After a private word with the directors, the detective in charge of the investigation gave the order for us to gather in the garden. John and Peter watched carefully, but they let the detective do his thing. After all, it wasn't like they had much choice

"Sorry to keep you, folks," the detective began, clapping his hands together. He was a short and stocky man, in his late-thirties with military short hair and a greying goatee.

"My name is Detective Adrian Isenblatter, and I'm here to talk to you about one of your ex-colleagues, Kerry Comstock. Now, I appreciate that it's been a while since his death, but I'm afraid that some disturbing new evidence has come to light, which has cast doubts on our initial investigation."

"What kind of evidence do you mean?" I asked. The detective touched his brow in a half salute.

"That's a good question," he said. "You seem like a smart guy. Now, I can't tell you all of the details, but I can tell you that we received an anonymous tip with some new information. Because of this, we're reopening our investigation. That's why I'm here to follow-up. I just want to talk to you, at least for the moment. There's nothing to worry about. We're just taking precautions, as we do with any crime."

"So it's a crime, now?" I asked.

Detective Isenblatter removed his cap and held it over his heart. "Unless our coroner is wrong, and our coroner is rarely wrong, it's the most serious crime of all," he said. "Murder."

***

The detective said no more, and he began to take us one by one into a private room, which turned out to be a disused storage room. I could picture the founders' faces as they sat at the big, wide boardroom table whilst the policeman conducted his interviews in a glorified wardrobe. Still, if the detective was put out by it, he didn't let it show. He simply stationed himself inside the room on a plastic chair and dealt with us one by one.

He worked methodically, and he interviewed everyone who worked at the company, whether they'd been here at the time or not. He also spoke to Nils and his men. From what I gathered, neither line of enquiry proved successful.

When it was my turn to go into the room, I felt terrified, even though I had nothing to hide. My hands started to sweat, and then I started shaking, and then I got so wound up about getting wound up that I started to wind myself up. I thought that I might look guilty, even though I was innocent, and that just made me look even guiltier. It was an unusual situation. I told them everything I could, whilst omitting my own suspicions and skirting around the low-level espionage that Nate and I were engaged in.

"Sit down, Mr. Roberts," Detective Isenblatter said as I entered the room. I wasn't convinced that the chair would take my weight, but I did as he asked and it seemed to cope, at least to begin with.

"How can I help you, Officer?" I asked.

The policeman frowned, but if he was trying to unnerve me, it didn't work. When he finally spoke, he said, "I'm going to be honest with you, Mr. Roberts. Let me explain the situation. We have reason to believe that at least one of your two founders is implicated in this murder. At this point, I have no reason to believe that anyone else in your team is involved. In my position, what would you do?"

I thought for a second, and then said, "In your position? I'd try to threaten everyone until someone, somewhere, knew something."

The detective grinned conspiratorially and leaned forward. "I'm glad we're on the same page, Mr. Roberts," he said. "If I were you, I'd start talking. And I'd start talking quickly…"

***

Detective Isenblatter learned nothing from me, but I swear he was smiling when I left. I wanted to talk to Flick, but she was still keeping her distance. The policeman left that afternoon, so I guess he got the information he was looking for. What he didn't realise was that his visit had an unexpected consequence.

It came in the form of a note from Nate, which he handed to me when I bumped into him in the bathroom. It simply said, "Usual place, 10:15." Still, I knew what he meant, so I kept my head down, nailed a couple of bug reports, drank a dozen cups of coffee and eventually, at about half past nine, I left the office and hopped into my

Tesla.

I arrived at the coffee shop early, so I ordered a cappuccino and sat down in my usual place. I was used to waiting – hell, life's a wait, when you look at it – so I didn't think twice when I finished my drink and checked the time on my phone.

I ordered myself another coffee, pulled a book out of my rucksack and waited for Nate to arrive.

**

I waited there until closing time, but Nate didn't show. He also didn't come to work the following day or the day after that. Nobody else seemed to notice, but I sure did. After that, it was the weekend, and then he didn't show up on the Monday or the Tuesday.

And then on the Wednesday, Detective Isenblatter paid us another visit, but this time he only wanted to speak to the founders. But that didn't stop him from giving us the lowdown before he marched the boys away to the "private room," which they were no longer laughing at now that they were sitting down inside it.

"Don't you worry, folks," the detective said. "This is part of a routine enquiry that's unrelated to the death of Kerry Comstock. I'm sorry to say that we might not be able to continue that investigation after all."

"Why not?" Flick asked. "You told us he was murdered!"

"We had information to that effect," the detective admitted. "But there have been some complications. That's why we're here, just in case your founders can help us with a few extra questions. Of course, if you think you can help us, then please do step forward."

He paused for a second and looked around at us, a

ragtag group of coders with a mission to change the world. I looked around to see if anyone was going to ask the obvious question. When I realised that no one was going to do it, I stepped forward.

"What happened?" I asked. "How come you're dropping the case?"

The detective whistled softly and stared me straight in the eye. "We're not dropping the case," he explained. "In fact, the case is very much still alive. It's just that this line of enquiry has come to an end, at least for now. We were acting on information received from an informant," he said. "He claimed to have further evidence which he had yet to show to us, evidence that he claimed would blow the case wide open and lead us to Mr. Comstock's killer."

"And the evidence didn't come up to scratch?" I asked.

"No," Isenblatter replied. "It's not that. The evidence never came to light, and we have reason to believe that our anonymous informant is the same person who was found behind Walmart with a knife through his heart."

***

I didn't push the matter, not in front of all of those witnesses, but I had a good idea of who the informant was. It had to be Nate. What else explained his disappearance? He'd said he had something to tell me. Perhaps it was connected to Kerry's death. And if it was to do with Kerry's death, then perhaps Kerry's killer was still on the prowl, trying to cover up their tracks.

I could deduce two further things if my initial assumption was correct. The first was that, if Nate was the informant and he wanted to speak to me, then Kerry's death must have had something to do with the company. The second was that if someone was prepared to kill to keep things quiet, I could be in danger. But I couldn't do anything about it. I wasn't prepared to talk to the cops, and who else could help me?

A couple of days after Isenblatter's visit, I had some sort of answer. Nate's profile went live on Former.ly with his cause of death listed as homicide. It caused quite the furore in the office, but the press failed to pick up on it. No one seemed worried that he was dead. After all, I was the only one who had ever spoken to him, and we weren't exactly friends, but there was a general unease about the death of another employee.

As for me, I just wanted to know what Nate was going to tell me. I scoured his Former.ly page for clues, but he hadn't been dumb enough to mention the investigation. In fact, his Former.ly profile painted his death in a consistent light with what his friends thought. They said he was an ex-programmer who was well-known and well-loved by the local community and that they couldn't understand how anyone could do such a thing.

But I could understand it. There was a lot at stake – money, reputations and lives on the line, my own included. There was a lot for me to think about.

CHAPTER TWENTY-FIVE

NATE'S DEATH WASN'T MENTIONED AGAIN, and John and Peter didn't bother to hire a replacement. But it was the calm before the storm. We formally announced the IPO on a Tuesday, and the press of the world went mental. Flick organised a music festival in Menlo Park. She'd been working on it for months and decided to repurpose it for the IPO. So we all boarded a bus in the morning to get down there before the show started.

It was a masterstroke for many reasons. John and Peter loved it because it kept the press away from the office, which made security easier. They could hire a third-party firm, instead of relying on Nils and his men and panicking the day before to make sure that everything was locked away. In fact, it was so well-planned that our confidence was high, and we were sure that nothing could go wrong. Famous last words. The day of the festival was warm and sunny with barely a cloud in the sky. We started drinking early, as soon as we got on the bus.

I was pretty drunk by the time that I arrived, and I was in no mood to hobnob with journalists. Luckily, I'd been chatting to Peter, and he felt the same as I did.

"I hate these things," he told me. "John's always been better at them than I am. For me, it's all about the product. If we build it, they will come. That's why John's doing all of the talking today. I'm just here for the booze and the bands."

"I couldn't agree more," I replied. Deep down, all I

could think about was what Abhi would have made of the show or what Kerry would have thought. Abhi would've loved it; Kerry would've hated it. They would've argued about it all day.

"I'm telling you, Dan," he said, helping himself to another can of Bud from the stash beneath the seats. "Life is just a game, and it's one I plan to win."

***

When the bus arrived at the festival site, Peter and I split from the rest of the group and made our way to the bar. The rest of the team was going backstage to hang out with the musicians and the tech elite. Not us – we weren't in the mood.

And so that was how Peter and I ended up sitting on camping chairs towards the back of the site, sharing a joint and sipping beer from plastic cups. I hadn't heard of most of the performers, but that was hardly the point. Flick had worked on the line-up, and she'd mined the data from our users to figure out what they wanted to hear. We were expecting twenty thousand people, but they were only there to show how powerful we'd become. The whole show was designed to cater to the journalists who'd been flown in at Former.ly's expense.

John and Flick took to the stage in the early evening to give a demo of the product on the main stage. By that point, Peter and I were so stoned that we'd stopped drinking, and we were expecting the demo to go down badly with the general public. But people loved it. Several thousand pissed-up revellers swallowed each of John's words like it was the second coming of Christ.

Then, Flick and John left the stage, and I fetched some tacos while some singer-songwriter played bubblegum pop as the sun died down. I couldn't stand her, but the crowd loved her. I sat with my back to her as she finished her set. I was just thinking about heading back to the compound when something unusual happened.

John was wheeled on to the stage in a coffin.

***

It turned out to be part of the plan. John was due to deliver his keynote from the comfort of his padded wooden box.

"Ladies and gentlemen," he began, as the big screens at the front of the stage flickered into life. "We've gathered you here for a reason. Well here it is, folks. You wanted an announcement, and you've got one. Former.ly is heading to the New York Stock Exchange!"

The crowd responded to the announcement with a cheer, but they were at a festival. They would've cheered anything.

"Former.ly has grown from strength to strength," John continued. "Even as I speak, new users are signing up to the site in record numbers. In some regions, we're in the top two or three social networks. In others, we're not far behind. Our most recent stats show two hundred and seventy million users. That's two hundred and seventy million people who've recognised their own mortality."

He shifted a little in the coffin and adjusted his tie, which was lying limply across the left half of his stomach. The camera angle made it look like he was standing up. I guessed, correctly, that the video was being simulcast on the web and that the eyes of the world were upon us.

"We're growing fast," John continued. "And we're profitable, consistently so. We're even running smoothly in China where even Google doesn't dare to follow us. Ladies and gentlemen, we have arrived."

Another scattering of applause. John waited for it to die down before he continued.

"Now that we're all grown up, we want to play with the big boys," he said. "That's why we're going public. We already answer to our users with the changes we make to the site. What difference does it make to us if our users become our shareholders?"

From the wings, four men in black suits – four men I'd never seen before in my life – stepped forward and walked over to the coffin. As one, they lifted it up on to their shoulders.

"And now, friends," John said, smiling. "It's time to enjoy our headline act. Love life while you've got it."

The lights went out, and three balls of fire spurted up into the air from the pyros. In the darkness, an orchestra was warming up. They played a funeral dirge while John was carried off stage.

***

"Have you seen this?" Flick scowled, slamming a newspaper down in front of me. I grunted and took a look at the article. It was a piece in the New York Times about the IPO.

"I have now," I said. "So what?"

"So what? Look at it!" She grabbed the paper, held it up in front of her face and started to read it.

"'CEO of tech start-up dies on stage,'" she began. "That's just the headline, Dan. It says, 'John Mayers, CEO of Palo Alto's Former.ly, announced today that the company will be publicly traded on the New York Stock Exchange. The announcement took place at a music festival in Menlo Park, which was organised by the company.'"

"So?"

"I haven't finished," she said. "Let me find it." She murmured to herself and skimmed her finger over the article, looking for her place. "Ah yes, here it is. 'Meanwhile, the online backlash has already begun with some users calling for a boycott of the site, claiming that Mayers showed disrespect to users by appearing in a coffin during the announcement.'"

"I still don't get it," I said. "Is that a bad thing? I thought you said there was no such thing as bad publicity."

"This is different," Flick replied. "Former.ly is different. It's about to become a publicly traded company. It's become bigger than us. Now, if one of us brings the company into disrepute..."

"Disrepute?"

"Whatever the hell you want to call it, then," she growled. "Either way, we're not playing around anymore."

I laughed, and she looked at me. "Listen, Dan," she whispered. "Whatever deal we had, forget about it. The only thing I care about is taking us public so I can dump my shares and get out of here."

Then, she walked away, leaving me there to think about Nate, and the message he'd tried, and failed, to leave me.

CHAPTER TWENTY-SIX

SOMETHING ABOUT NATE'S DEATH didn't sit right with me. I felt like I owed it to him to finish his work. So I tried, as best as I could, to continue the investigation. I went over my notes with a highlighter and started to pick out any inconsistencies, but I didn't really know what I was looking for or how I might know when I found it, so it was a long, tedious process.

I can't say I ever liked the guy, but I am a big believer in justice. I was never friends with Nate, like I was with Kerry and Abhi, but I did respect him, in a way. I felt like I owed it to him to find out the truth, if I could.

Two days later, it all kicked off again. I heard a commotion in the kitchen, so I went to find out what was happening. It turned out that Flick and Peter were being held apart by some of our junior staffers, and the air was black with "fucks" and "cunts."

I walked over to John, who was watching it like a reality TV show, and I asked him what was happening.

"Oh, that," he said, without looking away. "I have no idea." And then he asked me something that really tested my loyalties.

"Dan, you're going to have to get her out of here," he said. "Get her outside before she causes any more damage."

I looked at him, aghast. "Can't you get Nils to do it?" I asked. "Isn't that what you pay him for?"

John laughed. "I pay him for a lot of things," he said.

"And I pay you for a lot of things too. So get her out of here. I want her gone. And I want you to do it."

"Fuck you, John." This was from Flick, who was, for the moment, restrained. She turned her eyes from Peter to John like a missile locking on to its target. Then her shoulders sagged, and Nils's men relaxed their grip.

"Okay," Flick said. "Whatever. I'm done with this place. For good. Good luck holding it together, assholes."

She stormed off towards the exit, and we just stood there and watched her. I was about to go after her anyway to see if she was okay when John grabbed my arm and leant over to whisper in my ear.

"You follow her out, Dan," he said. "Make sure she leaves the building. For good."

"But–"

"Just do it, Dan. If you value your job."

***

Flick's career at Former.ly was over, and as the days and weeks began to melt away, we started to realise she was gone for good. I felt terrible, like I'd betrayed her. It hurt most when she asked me to pack her stuff into bags and drop it off to her, so she could ship it back to the UK.

I wanted to join her, but I couldn't. There was still so much to do. I just needed to hold on until the IPO. If all went well, we'd both be rich. And if it didn't, I had a backup plan. John and Peter were going to pay up, one way or another.

Meanwhile, Elaine had been hard at work, trying to build a global finance department from scratch. In China, we had three regional offices, and Chinese was the most widely spoken language on the service. We didn't release that information to the press of the Western world, though. They'd caused enough trouble already.

Flick wasn't the only casualty that week. Two days later, John and Peter summoned the team to make an announcement. We were all so busy that most of us brought our laptops, but the founders didn't care. As long as we were there and semi-listening, I guess it was good enough.

John kicked things off by thanking everyone for coming and launching into a brief presentation on the company's financials, with Elaine joining him towards the end to go over a few tricky figures.

"As you know," he said, "we're gearing up for our impending IPO. Many of our employees will become millionaires overnight, thanks to the shares that they hold, and many others will be well on their way."

John paused and scratched his nose before continuing. "Now, I'd like to take this opportunity to thank Elaine for all of the hard work that she's been doing. She's created a finance department from scratch, stopped us from going bankrupt, and helped us to navigate our way towards becoming a publically traded company. In fact, Elaine is so efficient that the vast majority of her work can now be automated. Can we get a round of applause?"

We acquiesced, and he waited for the noise to die down again. "Well," he said. "Now that we no longer need you, Elaine, you're fired. Thanks for your time, guys."

***

I was worried, about a lot of things. The founders were acting more eccentric than ever, security was on lockdown, and Nils and his men had doubled up patrols and taken on new recruits. There was a feeling in the air, like an electrical storm about to happen.

I didn't hear about the "accident" until two weeks later. Elaine had travelled back to the UK and settled easily into her old life; that is, until a truck driver ploughed into the back of her sedan, killing her instantly. Luckily, the press didn't cotton on to her connection with the company, and so she passed away unnoticed. But I thought I knew the truth, at last. Unfortunately, I didn't have any proof.

I needed some time to think, and I found myself idly cruising the streets of Palo Alto with nowhere to go but home. I thought I was driving at random, but I soon realised that I was heading towards the coffee shop where I used to meet Nate for his reports. Inside, I ordered myself a cappuccino and took a seat in the corner to be left alone with my thoughts. I'd brought my notebook along, but I spent the first hour sketching and colouring in the gaps between the lines.

I got up to get a refill, and someone took the opportunity to steal my seat. I scanned the room for somewhere else to sit, and inspiration hit me square in the face like Elaine's airbag. I was supposed to meet Nate on the same day that he died, and we always sat in the same place. It gave me an idea.

A couple of guys were already sitting there, but they paid me no mind when I got down on my hands and knees and started rooting around on the floor. Even if they'd sat and stared, it wouldn't have stopped me. Nothing ever does when I'm onto something.

I scanned around beneath the tablecloth and saw something which would change my life. A manila envelope was taped to the underside of the table, and it had a name on it. My name.

***

I left without drinking my coffee and drove around again to make sure I wasn't being followed before parking in an alleyway to inspect my prize. It was from Nate, and it was a fucking treasure trove. He had everything – printouts, photocopies, receipts, signatures and a flash drive with God knows what else on it.

I flicked through it quickly and then took another look in more detail. This was it. It was Nate's entire case, and he'd done a much better job of it than I had. I couldn't even begin to imagine how he'd found all this stuff.

Perhaps most damning of all were the early documents, handwritten by the two founders on the pages of a sketchbook. It outlined it all – their plan to create publicity by killing prominent users and to ensure their own safety by keeping their team of killers close at hand, in the form of Nils and his security personnel.

There were no records of individual killings or even of anything that could incriminate the founders for anything more than a twisted imagination. But it was still something that the police would want to see.

I should've given them the documents. I don't know why I didn't. Probably because I didn't trust them. I never had, ever since I was a kid and I got picked up for a couple of mild misdemeanours. But I didn't trust the founders either, especially now that I had a little extra evidence. It might not stand up in court, but it was good enough for me. Either way, I had a choice to make. Looking back, I guess you could say I chose badly.

With my mind made up, I stopped by an internet café to make scans and photocopies and then mailed them to as many addresses as I could remember. I didn't include a note or any indication as to what it was or who it was from. They wouldn't arrive until after the IPO, and by then I'd be long gone.

After that, I stashed the originals in a safety deposit box and drove back to the office. It was unusually cool for that time of year and the roads were empty, so I made good time, parked up, said hi to the guys and headed into my room.

I loaded up my laptop, typed out a quick e-mail and hit the send button and then passed out on my bed with my clothes on.

I woke up to a heavy knock at the door. Nils and his men were standing outside, cradling their firearms with determined looks in their eyes.

***

The security team marched me down a passage round the back of the boardroom and through a pair of double doors that I'd never been through. They were always locked and under armed guard. I quickly realised that I was inside the founders' private quarters – a rare honour. Nils escorted me into a small sitting room and gestured for me to take a seat. With no alternative, I complied and waited until the two founders were ushered into the room. They stared at me for a second and then turned to Nils and asked him to leave.

"Are you sure?" he asked, waving his weapon towards me.

"I'm sure," John said, smiling calmly. "I don't think he'll be any trouble. Isn't that right, Dan?"

I nodded, Nils left the room, and an uneasy silence descended. John and Peter stood opposite me with their arms crossed.

"Right," said John. "Let's get started, shall we? You know, and we know, so let's drop the bullshit. What's next?"

"Answers," I said. "I want to know why you did it."

"Did what?"

"Did you not see the e-mail?" I asked. "I've got you guys bang to rights."

John laughed, and Peter took over. "Of course we saw

the e-mail," he said. "But you can't prove anything. Sounds like it's your word against ours."

"Perhaps," I replied. "But then again, perhaps not. You don't need proof to destroy a reputation. Did Flick teach you nothing? What do you think the media will make of it?"

"You're bluffing," John said, but the colour of his face betrayed him.

"Want to bet?" I asked. "Why did you do it?"

John sighed and rubbed his eyes. "That's a complicated question, Dan. Most of the time, we had to; some of the time, we wanted to. And besides – Flick always told us that death sells a story, and we deal in it. What's one more corpse in a world of seven billion people?"

"Fuck you," I said. "Here's what's going to happen. I'm going to wait until the IPO, cash in my shares and then I'm out of here. You ought to get out of here too. Your secret won't last forever."

The two founders bowed their heads together for a moment and then turned to look at me. "How do you know we won't try to stop you?" Peter asked.

"If anything happens to me, Flick has a copy of the files, as do a dozen good friends of mine. If anything happens to me – if my plan goes awry in any way – they'll release them to the media. I guess I'm just hoping that you won't do anything stupid."

CHAPTER TWENTY-SEVEN

FROM THAT MOMENT ON, all I was worried about was getting paid and getting out of there. I stopped driving my car, I stopped writing my journal, and I did nothing to step out of line. I couldn't afford to. If I did, I'd be dead, and I knew it. I was only still alive because they trusted me – not out of choice but because they had to.

And so the evening before the IPO rolled around, as time tends eventually to do, and John and Peter flew their cronies in from all over the world to join them, including a half-dozen heavies from China, who were here on the orders of their government.

"Chinese is the language of the future," Peter explained. He spoke the language himself – not fluently, but well enough to get by without insulting his guests. "Business will be conducted in Chinese in the future," he predicted. "You mark my words."

Either way, I didn't want to mess around with those guys. Peter's Chinese was so-so, and John's was pretty poor, and I hadn't got a fucking clue what they were talking about. I didn't like the look of the Chinese businessmen, either. They were built and dressed to kill, and even Nils and his men would struggle to contain them if a fight kicked off.

Luckily, they seemed friendly enough, and so I wasn't too worried when I was called into a meeting with our visitors. I'd been working on some patches, which I was pretty sure broke international copyright laws, so I was perfectly happy to down tools and to walk into the founders' office, back through those double doors, to discuss things.

The problem was, I just didn't care anymore. The truth would come out eventually, and I had nothing left to live for. Sarah was gone, Flick was back in the UK, and everyone else was dead. People called me brave, but I wasn't brave. I was just fucking stupid. I was in over my head and I wanted out. Just one more day to go and I was a free man. A rich, free man.

***

And then it happened. It was never a good sign when you were summoned to see the founders, and it was even worse when you had to go through the security door. Nils led me straight through. He didn't bother to warn me.

The visiting Chinese dignitaries were battered and bloody, bound and gagged and collapsed across the sofa. I don't know what made me feel worse – the copper smell of blood or the way that Peter winked at me when I entered. I stared at him, open-mouthed. I guess shit like that affects you more when you're not used to it. John and Peter looked tired, bored, even.

John nodded at Nils, and he handed over his firearm and left the room without another word. For a second, I thought John was going to shoot me, but he checked the safety and handed it over.

"Go ahead," he said. "Take it." I took it, and Peter laughed.

"Feels good, doesn't it?" he said. "Now, prove that we can trust you. Shoot them. Put them out of their misery."

I hesitated, and John walked over and put his arm around my shoulder. "Go on," he said. "Do it. What's the worst that can happen?"

I thought of all of the things that could happen, and none of them appealed to me. Then again, who knew what would happen if I refused? I removed the safety and aimed the gun at the two men. I felt my way around the trigger and became one with it. Even now, I can still feel it, like a phantom limb after an amputation.

"Do it," John said.

I hesitated, aimed again and then lowered the barrel of the gun. "No," I said. "Fuck you, guys. I'm done. I'm out of here."

I put the safety back on and put the gun down. Nobody moved, and I edged slowly towards the door. As soon as I'd crossed the threshold, I ran like hell.

As I reached the outside of the complex, I heard gunshots.

***

With nowhere to go, I grabbed my journal, my passport, my stash of evidence and a change of clothes, and then hopped in the Tesla and drove around at random, homing steadily in towards the café. I ordered a coffee and sat down at the table, gently cradling it as I tried to gather my thoughts. There were a lot of them, and all of them were jumbled.

With the first cup out of the way, I went back to my car to pick up my laptop, ordered another coffee and sat back down. Whilst the coffee cooled, I loaded up the machine and dashed out a couple of e-mails with the only contact information I could find. I had to try.

I shut the laptop down and tried to relax. Unfortunately, I tried to relax by watching the TV, and what I saw was far from relaxing. Nestled amongst a couple of upbeat local news items was a brief piece on a breaking news story, and I realised I was looking at a photo of John.

"An anonymous tip off to both the media and the police force has led to the arrest of the two founders of Palo Alto-based social networking site Former.ly," the anchor explained.

"As of yet, there's been no official word from the police force or from the company, except to confirm the arrest of the two men, but the e-mail that we received claims that John Mayers, the company's CEO, has been arrested for the murder of four of the company's former employees - Abhijeet Desi, Kerry Comstock, Nate Hooper and Elaine Dell. He's also being questioned in relation to the deaths of two visiting Chinese diplomats.

"Peter Bow, Mr. Mayers's co-founder, appears to have been arrested as part of an international effort involving the British Metropolitan Police Force. According to our informant, he's yet to be charged but under suspicion of grand larceny and embezzlement. This is a breaking news story which is still developing. We'll provide you with further updates as and when we receive additional information."

The news reporter handed back over to her co-presenter, who embarked on a story about a fire at an industrial complex, and I got up to order another drink.

***

I wasn't expecting the cops to find me so quickly, although I knew it was inevitable – for all that, I wasn't exactly hiding. They walked into the café like they owned the place, and then they marched straight up to me.

"Daniel Roberts?" one of the cops asked. "Mind if we ask you a few questions?"

"Am I under arrest?" I asked.

"Not yet," he replied.

"How did you find me?"

The policeman laughed. "Mr. Roberts, if we want to find someone, we find them. The chief wants to talk to you about Former.ly Come on. We'll fill you in at the station."

They didn't use their siren, which would have been cool, but I guess they only use that when someone's done something wrong. I didn't think I had. In fact, I didn't know what I'd done. I found out when I got to the station. I caught a glimpse of Peter on my way to the interrogation room, but I wisely avoided eye contact.

"Right, Mr. Roberts," Detective Isenblatter said, as he pulled out a chair for me to sit on. "Do you know why you're here?"

"No," I said. Honesty was the best policy, right? "Do tell me."

"Well," he continued. "I guess you already heard the news about your buddies at Former.ly?"

"They're not my buddies," I said. "They are, or they were, my bosses. But yeah, I heard about it."

"That's not how they tell it," he replied. "In fact, you've been fingered as an accomplice."

"Who said that?"

"It doesn't matter," Detective Isenblatter said. "What's important is that you tell us everything you know, and fast. If you help us with our investigation, it could stop you from going to jail. You see, we know things – things you'd probably prefer us not to know about. We know, for example, that you suspected your former employers of breaking the law in a number of different ways. Why didn't you ever come forward?"

"I never had any proof," I replied.

The detective sighed and crossed his arms. "See," he

said. "As much as I'd like to believe you, Mr. Roberts, I don't. You see, we had an informant working on the inside – Nate Hooper. I think you knew him. He told us everything you knew at every stage of the investigation. Just as we were about to make an arrest, he was murdered. We had our suspicions at the time, but now we have the evidence that we need to prove that John Mayers was the mastermind behind it."

"You might have your proof," I said. "But I didn't have mine."

"Perhaps not," the policeman said. "If you're as innocent as you say you are, then you won't mind if our officers take a quick look through your laptop."

"Do what you have to," I replied.

"Oh, we will. Mr. Roberts, I think you knew exactly what was going on, but you didn't want to cause any trouble ahead of the company going public. Come tomorrow morning, you'll be a rich man."

"Not anymore," I said.

"So let's see," Detective Isenblatter continued. "That gives us a pretty wide choice of charges to level, but let's start with the biggie –harbouring known criminals. We could probably slap you with aiding and abetting and accessory to murder if we wanted to. What do you have to say about that, then?"

"I didn't do anything wrong," I insisted.

Detective Isenblatter just looked at me. "We found a gun in the complex," he said. "With two sets of fingerprints on it. One belonged to John Mayers, and the other set is unknown. So, are you going to provide us with your prints, or are we going to have to arrest you to get them?"

I said nothing.

CHAPTER TWENTY-EIGHT

IN THE END, I confessed to some of the charges and pleaded my innocence when it came to others. I told the cops what I could, feeding them a mixture of lies, half-truths and occasional suppositions – whatever I thought they wanted to hear – and went through my options with my lawyer. Eventually, I traded in my envelope of evidence for a reduction in the number of charges, on his advice. I lucked out, and my court-appointed lawyer knew what he was talking about. If I ever get arrested again, I hope my luck still holds.

When the news broke, the IPO was halted pending federal investigation, another world first for Former.ly. I never did see any money from those shares. Still, nothing ventured…

John and Peter were both sentenced before me. John got twenty-five to life, and Peter was slapped with a minimum of twelve years. I wasn't in the courtroom. I testified against them at a deposition on the condition that I wouldn't have to attend the trial. But I read about it in the tabloids. I heard that they showed no remorse, which didn't surprise me.

When my trial rolled around, I barely said a word. My attorney handled most of it, and I'd been drilled beforehand so that when I was cross-examined, I knew exactly what to say. I thought we were on to a winner.

And then the sentence was read out. Three years behind bars, maybe two on good behaviour. I'd already served some of the time because I couldn't afford to post bail, so I was already halfway through my sentence without even trying. Fucking, yay.

Still, my attorney seemed happy with the result. Let's face it. It was his job. On the whole, I tried to look on the bright side, but it was hard.

At least they let me keep my journal.

***

It was seventeen months since my arrest, and I was still counting down the days 'til my release. I'd kept my head down and served my time just like everyone else, but I was high-profile. I didn't want them to make an example of me.

I hadn't seen either of the founders since the day I left the gun behind, but I heard they were doing well. I hadn't seen Flick either, although I'd heard from her. She kept her distance for a while – she said she wanted to get her head straight and to forget about Former.ly for good – but that all changed about a month ago when she called me at the penitentiary.

"Hey," she said. "It's been a while."

"It has," I agreed. Then I waited for her to speak. It was a habit you picked up quickly in a place like this.

"How's life treating you?" she asked.

"How do you think?" I scowled.

"Don't worry. It's almost over. Come and find me when you get out of here," she said. "We've got some unfinished business to attend to."

***

A week before my release, Former.ly hit the news again. I heard about it on the battered old TV set in the common room. With nothing better to do, most of the cons whiled away the evenings watching the news channels and playing poker for cigarettes. I was no different. By the time of my release, I'd collected over four thousand cigarettes. As a non-smoker, that made me a rich man.

I saw the segment on the evening news. Peter was dead. He'd been found in the showers with a toothbrush in his throat. No motive was given, but I had a good guess. He could wind people up until they were about to break, and he was a high-profile target too. A lot of those guys had nothing to lose. When you're already a lifer, what harm can an extra twenty years do?

His funeral took place a couple of days before I got out, but I wouldn't have gone. Turns out that nobody else went either. There were no reports of it at all, as far as I could tell, although Flick was gutted to miss it because she wanted "to make sure that the bastard was really dead."

When they finally let me out, there was no one there to meet me, so I hitched my way back to the city. I made my way to an internet café, sent out a couple of e-mails and then waited.

***

I found an unlikely saviour. Half of my e-mails bounced back, and nobody else bothered to reply. I was asking for a lot, after all. I needed someone to cover the cost of a flight home, as well as a place to stay when I got there. I had nothing – no friends, no money and no hope.

And then I got an e-mail from Sarah with an offer. She was still working at TheNextWeb, but she'd worked her way up to become the site's editor. Her offer sounded reasonable enough to me, and it could help us both out.

"Hey, Dan," she'd written. "Long time, no speak.

How've you been? I hope life wasn't too hard on you.

"Listen, thanks for your e-mail. I understand you're in a bit of a bind, and I might be able to help – at least, my company might. Here's the deal, we can wire you some cash to keep you going for now, just to tide you over until we get you back to the UK, but we'll be sending you a contract that we want you to sign.

"Basically, the offer is this. We fly you home and cover your accommodation for six weeks, depending on how useful you are to us, and in return, you give us exclusive rights to your story. We're going to make you famous, Dan, and TheNextWeb will ride the waves."

I didn't have much choice in the matter, so I took her up on the offer. Luckily, I still had all of my journals, as well as a copy of the files. I started work on a series of articles before I'd even signed the contract. The articles took off, and three of them ended up in the site's top five performers of the year.

As a result, they took me on full-time, despite my criminal record. It was what the readers wanted, and it worked out well for everyone, including Sarah. Our past was just that – the past. She'd started dating a lawyer. Fair play to her, their combined wage put mine to shame, but I had enough to get by, and that was good enough for me.

Besides, it was nowhere near as stressful as Former.ly.

***

I put down the advance on my paycheque to rent an unfurnished apartment, one which was available immediately and with cheap rent that made up for its crappy interior and bad location. I kitted it out with basic furniture and tried to make the place seem like home.

One evening, after work, Sam – the policeman – paid me

a visit. He was in uniform, and he pulled up outside the apartment in his panda car. One of his colleagues waited behind in the passenger seat as I let him into the living room. I offered him a cup of tea, but he declined.

"Can't," he said. "I'm on duty. Listen, Dan, I can't stop to chat. I just wanted to let you know before the press picks up on it. It'll be all over the papers tomorrow."

"What will?"

"The arrest," Sam replied. "The one that we just made. We've just taken Sarah in for questioning. She's suspected of involvement in Alex's death. She lied to us, Dan. She told us she was with you, but she wasn't, was she?"

"No, she wasn't," I said. "But that doesn't mean she did it. Where's the motive?"

"That's easy," Sam said. "She was cheating on you, Dan. She was seeing someone else from the office, and Alex knew all about it. And he had an obsession. According to the office gossip, Alex told her he loved her, she told him to get lost and he lost his mind. He wanted revenge. He was planning on telling you everything, and Sarah didn't want that to happen. Besides, with Alex gone, she was the logical choice to take over his role, which I notice is exactly what happened."

"And you can prove all this?"

"Of course I can," the policeman replied, smiling. "If I couldn't, we wouldn't have taken her in. John and Peter both had an alibi, and the modus operandi – that's how the killer acted – was different. They used poison, and poison is usually a woman's weapon. John and Peter were much less subtle, at least in their methods, if not in their attempt to escape detection. Sarah, on the other hand, has motive, opportunity and no alibi."

I looked at him, astonished. "You're telling me that Sarah killed Alex? Not John and Peter? Are you sure?"

"As sure as I can be," he replied. "But I suppose we'll see whether we can convince a jury of her peers in the courtroom. The evidence is pretty compelling, though. And besides, I know a lot about the Former.ly case, and this one's unrelated, I'd bet my life on it."

"How come you know so much?" I asked.

Sam smiled. "That's easy," he said. "The Metropolitan Police has been working closely with the Palo Alto Police Department. We provided them with resources and information about your operations in London, and Palo Alto PD planted a mole inside the company."

I sat in silence for a couple of seconds, deep in thought. Eventually, I asked: "Why are you telling me this?"

Sam laughed and made his way over to the door. "It's a warning, Dan," he said. "A warning and a reminder. You've served your time, for now. Don't do anything stupid. Let bygones be bygones. Forget Former.ly and focus on the future."

"I plan to," I murmured, as he saw himself out.

***

It was dark and it was raining, and I was tapping away at my machine, checking out some of the comments on my latest articles. I'd already managed to mess the place up with empty beer cans and takeaway boxes, and I wasn't in the mood for company. And then, of course, the doorbell rang.

I looked out through the bolt-hole, but all I could make out was a hooded figure, dressed in black. I put the chain on the door and opened it up, just a crack. My visitor reached up to lower her hood, unleashing a wave of blonde hair. For the first time in a long time, her smile extended to her eyes.

"Hey, Dan," Flick said, rushing over to hug me. "Welcome back to reality. Can I come in?"

I smiled and stepped aside and then locked the door behind us.

THE END

ACKNOWLEDGMENTS

First and foremost, thanks to Dan Webb and Abhijeet Patil for letting me steal their names, and thanks to Dan, Abhi and Geza Dezsi for accidentally teaching me about professional web development. Hannah Parkinson taught me more than she'd admit to, too.

Credit is also due to everyone at fst – in particular, to Mark Howard, Craig Watson and Otto Marples for providing me with plenty of material to steal, as well as a steady income.

Finally, huge thanks to my family and friends, who have always been my biggest supporters. I can't name them all, but here are just a few of them: Donna Woodings, Carl Woodings, Heather and Dave Clarke, Alan and Olga Woodings, Amanda de Grey, Neil Denham, Dave Ford, Jesse James Freeman, Thom Mutch, Lucy Burrows, Nick Reffin, Rebecca Groves, Clive Whitelock, Steve Woodcock and everyone else who takes the time to read my books. And that includes you. Thanks!

JOIN THE CONVERSATION

Thanks for reading Former.ly! Whether you loved the book or you hated it, I want to know what you think. Join the conversation by tweeting @DaneCobain.

danecobain.com

twitter.com/danecobain

facebook.com/danecobainmusic

MORE GREAT READS
FROM DANE COBAIN

No Rest for the Wicked (Supernatural Thriller) When the
Angels attack, there's No Rest for the Wicked. Cobain's
debut novella, a super-natural thriller, follows the story of
the elderly Father Montgomery as he tries to save the
world—or at least, his parishioners—from mysterious,
spectral assailants.

Eyes Like Lighthouses When the Boats Come Home (Poetry)
Eyes Like Lighthouses is Dane Cobain's first book of poetry,
distilled from the sweat of a thousand memorised
performances in this reality and others. It's not for the faint-
hearted.

Discover more books
at **danecobain.com**.

Printed in Great Britain
by Amazon

87572230R10114